Forged by Fire

Danger in Destiny
Book 9

Melanie D. Snitker

Forged by Fire
Danger in Destiny: Book 9
By Melanie D. Snitker

Dallionz Media, LLC
P.O. Box 5283
Abilene, TX 79608

Cover Art: Dallionz Media, LLC

For permission requests, please contact the author at the email below or through her website.

Melanie D. Snitker
melanie@melaniedsnitker.com
www.melaniedsnitker.com

For my friend,
Steph Dowlen.
Your friendship is a
true blessing, and
I'm so thankful for you!

Chapter One

F irefighter Leslie Granger cast a longing look at the chocolate cream pie sitting on the counter at the fire department. She'd been ready to make the first cut when the alert went out calling both crews of Company B to respond to a fire. She could almost taste the sweet chocolate and whipped cream confection, but it would have to wait.

She slapped the cover back on the pie and slid it into the fridge before taking off at a jog.

Her friend and fellow firefighter, Danny Bracken, laughed at her. "It'll still be here when we get back."

The whole station knew of her love for all things chocolate, but it was Danny who claimed that, if she didn't get her fix each day, she'd turn into some kind of monster. One he doubted any of them would want to cross.

Leslie wasn't necessarily addicted to it, but she did eat something with chocolate most days. Still, ever since Danny's comment, she'd made sure to bring a package of M&Ms or something similar to work each day. Whenever someone annoyed her, she'd make a show of pulling them out and popping a few in her mouth as though they truly were the miracle cure when it came to calming her down.

"It'd better be."

She and the rest of Company B quickly donned their gear as Chief Menendez raised his voice to be heard over the noise. "All right, people. We've got a fire alarm sounding at a warehouse in the industrial district. Flames are visible. There's also a report that someone may be trapped inside." He turned to look at Curtis Whitman, their resident paramedic. "Whitman, you'll be joining company B."

"Yes, sir." He sprang to action, getting ready in record speed.

Leslie glanced at the clock on the wall. It was after six on a Monday evening. Hopefully, no one was in the warehouse, but there was certainly no guarantee of that. Especially considering many of the businesses in the area kept the warehouses running twenty-four hours a day over multiple shifts.

She sent up a silent prayer that everyone was safe.

The size of the building and the fact that a fire had been verified was why both the engine and ladder were being sent. There were a lot of warehouses out there, and the contents could vary greatly. It was crucial they got the fire under control as quickly as possible before something toxic caught fire or it had a chance to spread.

Lieutenant Chet Holden, the ladder company officer she reported directly to, jabbed a thumb at the truck behind him. "You heard the chief. Let's go, people."

They used to only have two engine companies at Station #2. But two months ago, they'd expanded and added a brand-new station and the ladder truck. Leslie considered it an honor to be part of the new ladder company. It also meant they were closer to the south part of town. Right now, if that weren't the case, it would take an extra ten minutes or more for a ladder truck from another station to get to the burning warehouse.

Engineer Bryce Keyes was the first to get the rest of his equipment on and swung into the driver's seat.

Within seconds, Leslie, Danny, Curtis, and firefighter Jin Cho were seated and ready to go. They led the way down the street, the engine and its company not far behind them.

Sirens broke the silence, announcing their approach to any vehicles up ahead. Bryce expertly steered them through the maze of roads that led them to the industrial part of town. Even before they reached the warehouses, she could see a plume of dark smoke rising into the dimming evening sky.

The chief's voice came over the radio. "The warehouse primarily stores paper that's manufactured in a plant nearby. The good news is, there isn't much in the way of hazardous material to deal with. The bad news is, the entire building is basically filled with fuel to keep this monster going."

They traveled through a parking lot and into another that bordered the warehouse. A group of people stood to the side, many of them filming the fire on their cell phones or talking into them.

One end of the gigantic structure was fully involved all the way to the roof. It was impossible to tell how much of the inside was consumed by fire.

Bryce stopped the truck, and everyone disembarked as two men ran up to them.

"Oh, thank goodness." The taller, older man waved at the warehouse. "We thought everyone was out, but two people are unaccounted for. Chris, one of our security guards, and Sarah, who was updating the inventory lists. They may still be inside."

The other man, his thin hair pulled back into a low ponytail at the base of his neck, held up his cell phone. "Should I try to reach their families? See if they went home early?"

Chet stepped forward. "Please do. We're going to send teams in to clear the area just in case they're still in there. But if we can confirm they aren't, then we can put more focus on putting out the fire. See if we can keep this from being a total loss."

The rest of Company B left the fire engine and joined them. Lieutenant Robby Warren, the engine company officer, gave Chet a nod. "We'll lay hose lines and get a water supply established."

"I'm going to send in two teams to look for people who may not have made it out." Chet pointed to Leslie and Danny. "Granger and Bracken, you'll be team one. Whitman, you're with Cho and Keyes. Once we know the situation inside, we can adjust our plans." Chet pointed to the entrance. "Keep your heads on a swivel."

Leslie hoped and prayed that the missing individuals would be located quickly.

The four firefighters put on the rest of their gear, including helmets and their self-contained breathing apparatuses. Once ready, they entered at the end of the warehouse opposite the visible fire. As a safety measure, the electricity had been shut off as soon as they'd arrived. Thanks to the expansiveness of the building, headlamps on their helmets were necessary.

The beams of lights illuminated the darkness around them. There wasn't much smoke at their level at first, but Leslie knew it could change quickly.

The two teams branched off, and Leslie and Danny started calling out.

"Chris! Sarah! Can you hear us?"

Leslie felt like her voice was being swallowed between her mask and the dark vastness of the warehouse. She listened intently, hoping one of the people they were looking for might call out for help. Instead, they were met with an eerie quietness that seemed strange given the fire raging on the other end of the warehouse.

They systematically made their way through their side of the warehouse in the direction of the flames, going through it as quickly and as efficiently as they could.

The smoke grew thicker, and the engine crew reported that one end of the warehouse was already fully involved, and that the room there was not structurally sound.

"Keyes and Granger, I need your teams to finish and get out of there as fast as possible."

"Yes, sir." Bryce's response was clipped. "We may have something here. Stand by."

Leslie and Danny exchanged a glance. She prayed Bryce's team had found the missing individuals. She couldn't explain why, but a sense of dread had settled into the pit of her stomach, like a ball that refused to budge.

An orange glow flickered in the distance.

Bryce's voice came back over the radio. "We've located Chris. Working our way back to the exit now."

Leslie released a sigh of relief. Now, if they could just find Sarah.

"Hey!" Danny nudged her arm and pointed. Ahead of them, a hallway led further on, choked by smoke. A firefighter approached, his arms crossing in the air above his head as he tried to get their attention.

Between the distance, smoke, and the headlamp shining light at them, it was impossible to tell who it was.

The firefighter motioned them to follow him and turned around again.

"What's going on?" Leslie spoke into the radio, hoping to get a heads up on the situation. Did Bryce and Jin need help getting Chris out of the building?

"Granger? Can you repeat that?" Chet's voice pierced the silence.

Danny led the way down the hallway, and Leslie followed close behind him. If there was one thing that'd been drilled into her since the beginning of her training, it was that you never took your eyes off your partner.

"It looks like Keyes and his team needs some assistance. We're working our way there now."

They got to the end of the hallway and turned right.

Bryce's voice came over the radio. "Granger. Cho, Whitman, and I already made it out with Chris. You and Bracken are clear to leave."

If they weren't in the building anymore, then who were they following? Had one of the other teams come in from the other side of the warehouse?

They rounded the corner and Danny stopped so quickly that Leslie nearly ran right into his back. "What is it?"

The firefighter they were following stood in the center of the room, a gun in his now-bare hand. Thanks to the smoke and the headlamps, it was impossible to see through the mask to make out the face on the other side. Her gaze flicked to where the name tag should've been, but it was missing completely.

"Hey, let's just calm down here." Danny slid to his left, effectively putting himself between Leslie and the gun. "What's your name?"

"Report!" Chet's voice held an equal measure of command and concern.

Leslie lowered her voice. "We've got a situation here. We're being held at gunpoint."

"Acknowledged. I'm contacting DPD right now."

That was little comfort when the building was literally burning down around them, and her partner was facing a gunman they knew nothing about.

"Come on, man." Danny took a step forward. "Let's get out of here and have a conversation."

The firefighter's helmet slowly moved back and forth. The headlamp illuminated walls, water bottles stacked on the floor nearby, and finally focused on Danny. "No. It's too late for that." He fired the gun, the sound piercing the air and making Leslie jump. Immediately, he turned and strode out of the room.

"Danny?" Leslie sidestepped around her partner just as he slumped to the ground. "No!" A furtive glance at the doorway assured her the shooter wasn't there. She fell to her knees beside her partner. "Shots fired. Danny's been hit." She leaned over him to peer into his mask. His eyes were closed. She shook him gently, alarmed by the pool of blood that was beginning to form beneath his body. He didn't respond.

With all his gear, there was no way she could stop the flow. She needed to get him out. Now.

"Danny isn't responding. I'm going to bring him out. I'm not sure where the shooter went. He looked just like one of us wearing full firefighter gear, but there's no name on the jacket."

7

Danny's PASS device started to sound the pre-alarm. If he didn't move soon, the full alarm would go off. It was a safety device that helped others find a fallen firefighter when visibility was low. The sound itself was a reminder of her partner's unknown condition. Leslie moved the device to keep it from going off fully.

"Got it. Granger, Whitman and I are on the way back to you guys." Bryce's voice was tight. No doubt the alarm had been heard over the radio as well.

"Understood. I'm bringing him out." She was trained to be able to carry a man out of a burning building if it were ever necessary. She tried to push the fact that it was Danny out of her mind and focused on the task at hand. With a groan, she managed to roll his body and get him onto her shoulders. His lack of response worried her even further as she summoned every ounce of strength she had to carry him out of the room.

Smoke billowed around her, and the light from her headlamp barely penetrated it enough to see where she was going. With each labored step Leslie took, she half expected the killer to come out of the shadows. Her priority had to be getting Danny out of the warehouse. There was no way to know how long he had before he bled out.

"God, help me get him out of here in time. Please help him to keep breathing." Her prayer was whispered in desperation as her partner's weight made it a challenge to maneuver through the warehouse with any kind of speed.

She stumbled into an open area and stopped suddenly when two bouncing lights appeared before her, nearly losing her footing.

Two firefighters materialized as the lights drew closer, but it wasn't until Leslie could read their names on the jackets that she started moving again. "Thank God."

Bryce didn't hesitate to reach for Danny. He easily took the man's weight onto his shoulders and led the way. Whitman gave Leslie's back a hard pat and brought up the rear. Together, they continued through the thick smoke for the exit, and Leslie prayed they wouldn't come face-to-face with the shooter before they found it.

Chapter Two

Smoke billowed from the broken windows in the warehouse. Police Officer Clint Baker wasn't going to pretend to know exactly how the fire department approached a blaze like this, but even he could tell the fire was anything but contained.

And somewhere in there, Leslie was trying to get her partner out with a shooter on the loose.

The last thing Clint wanted to do was wait outside for them to show up. Instead, his instinct was to charge in, locate Leslie and her partner, and escort them out safely. Except he wasn't an idiot. He knew very well doing that with no equipment or training would mean he'd be the one needing some to drag him out of a burning building.

Officers were positioned around the perimeter of the warehouse watching for the shooter to exit. Meanwhile, Clint waited near Lieutenants Holden and Warren. He could hear what they were saying to the other member of their companies but wasn't privy to the side of the conversation coming from inside the building.

Lieutenant Holden gave a sharp nod. "Understood." He

turned to Clint. "Our other team has located Granger and Bracken. They're on the way out."

Lieutenant Warren waved to get the attention of the waiting ambulance. "Get ready. They'll be out any minute."

The EMTs lowered a stretcher from the back of the ambulance. Medical gear hung from bags over their shoulders.

Clint spoke into the radio on his shoulder that connected him with the other officers in the area. "Be advised that we have four firefighters on their way out. At least one gun shot wound. We need to identify everyone exiting before they're allowed to leave the premises."

"Understood."

So far, the shooter hadn't emerged from the warehouse —a building that had to be burning down around him. Had the guy gone into this with a plan to escape the blaze? Or was it a random act of violence? The likelihood that the shooter had no intention of escaping alive flitted across Clint's mind.

The possibilities threw everything into question, including the source of the fire itself. Was it a convenient distraction, or was it set to cover up a premeditated crime?

Someone yelled, "We've got movement!"

Clint watched the door as four people poured out with the smoke, one of the firefighters draped over the shoulder of another. Immediately, the fire medic helped ease the injured fire fighter from Keyes' shoulders and placed him on the ground.

Clint joined the two lieutenants as well as the EMTs as they jogged forward to assist. The lieutenants quickly checked the identification of the firefighters.

"It's my company. We're good." Holden gave Clint a definitive nod.

Leslie took her helmet off and dropped it on the ground as she removed her regulator. "Is he alive? I couldn't tell if he was alive or not. I just had to get him out of there. The fire and the shooter..." She looked up and around, her eyes wide, until she saw Clint. "Did you find the man who shot him?"

Clint let the other officers in the area know that the four firefighters were legit and that the shooter was still in the wind. He put a hand on Leslie's shoulder. "I'm afraid not. He hasn't emerged from the building. We have officers posted all around the perimeter waiting for when he does."

"I don't have a pulse. Starting compressions." Whitman climbed onto the stretcher, straddled the injured firefighter, and began CPR.

An EMT fit a mask over the firefighter's face and used a bag to feed precious oxygen into his lungs.

Whitman stopped compressions long enough to check the man's pulse and shook his head. "Nothing."

Another EMT gave a definitive nod. "Preparing the defibrillator."

Leslie watched the medical personnel work. She cupped her elbows and held her arms as close to her chest as her gear would allow. Her jaw was clenched, and her gaze never left her partner.

Clint's heart went out to her. He'd known her for a few years now, but only professionally. They'd crossed paths many times when it came to different cases or emergency situations. He'd been tempted—more than once—to see if she'd be interested in going to dinner with him. But the timing never seemed right.

Now, he wanted to offer his support. Let her know that he was praying for her partner. For her, too. Goodness knew it had to have been horrible to witness what she had.

But someone from her company stood on each side of her, almost shoulder to shoulder. She probably had all the support she needed.

Instead, he sent up another silent prayer.

Please, God, guide the hands of Curtis and the EMTs. Give them the wisdom to know what to do. Help us catch the shooter.

The EMT shocked Bracken twice before one of them gave a satisfied nod. "I've got a pulse." They continued to assist with his breathing as they rolled him toward the ambulance.

Leslie whirled to face one of the lieutenants, her hazel eyes wide and filled with emotion.

"Go." Lieutenant Holden tilted his head toward the ambulance. "The rest of us will be there as soon as we can."

She barely took the time to nod before she was jogging to catch up with them and got into the ambulance, disappearing when the doors closed behind her.

Clint needed to get her statement. See if she could tell him anything at all about the shooter. As far as he was concerned, with Bracken heading into surgery, she was their only witness.

They still hadn't seen the shooter exit the building. Assuming the guy was still inside, Clint didn't like the idea of Leslie sitting at the hospital alone. He called in and spoke with Police Chief Arnold Dolman and was relieved when he received permission to head over to the hospital to speak with Leslie. After all, if she had any description at all, it would help them spot the killer if he ditched the gear and tried to walk out in plainclothes.

At the hospital, Clint entered through the main door and was immediately hit with the scent of antiseptic, some kind of pasta being served in the cafeteria down the hall, and many voices as people got directions or checked in for a procedure.

He found Leslie in the waiting area of the emergency room. She'd shed the rest of her gear, which she'd piled on the floor and a nearby chair and was standing in a pair of black pants and a dark green, short sleeve shirt. Her rich brown hair fell like a waterfall past her shoulders.

Hope lifted her features the moment she spotted him. "Please tell me you guys caught the shooter."

"Not yet."

The moment the words left his lips, the hope on her face gave way to worry.

"We will." He spoke with confidence, hoping that it would help put her at ease. "How's your partner doing?"

Leslie glanced at the information desk. "They're getting x-rays so they can see exactly what they're dealing with before taking him into surgery." She swallowed as tears flooded her eyes. She blinked them away furiously as though allowing them to fall might show some kind of weakness.

"Were they able to give you any kind of prognosis yet?"

"No. Just that he's in critical condition and they were going to do everything they could." She shrugged. "His wife, Becca, is on her way. She was visiting her parents in Dallas. I think they're driving her in. Danny and Becca... They're expecting their first baby in February."

"I'm sorry, Leslie." A firefighter, just like a police officer, knew the risks of the job. It was understood that there was a chance they could be injured or killed in the line of duty. Still, of all the dangers Danny Bracken could've faced today, getting shot never should've been one of them.

"It's all so senseless. I don't understand why it happened at all."

Clint touched her elbow and gently led her to a corner of the waiting room where they could sit and talk and not be overheard. "Can you tell me exactly what happened? Any detail, no matter how small, may help us figure out who the shooter is."

Her gaze darted to the nurses' station as though she were afraid she might miss an update. The nurse sitting there looked up at the same time and gave her a subtle nod. Only then did Leslie relax against the back of her chair a little.

She scrubbed her hands over her face. "Everything happened so fast. None of it makes any sense."

The poor woman looked exhausted. No doubt the adrenaline that'd carried her this far was beginning to ebb.

Clint had plenty of experience speaking with witnesses and helping them focus their thoughts by asking specific questions. He might know Leslie, but that didn't make his approach any different.

"Can you describe the shooter? You mentioned it was a man. How did you know? Was he taller or shorter than you?"

Leslie used one hand to massage her forehead with the tips of her fingers. "I heard his voice. But even before that, I knew he was a man. Because of his stature, I guess. I'm five foot seven, and he was at least four inches taller than me. I truly thought it was Bryce Keyes when I first saw him." She held one of her hands out in front of her. "He wasn't wearing a glove on his right hand. The one he used to hold the gun. His skin was a lighter color. I didn't notice the shade. He could have been white, Latino, or Asian, but he wasn't Black."

"Did you ever see his face?"

"No. Not more than an outline. He didn't have facial

hair, but then no active firefighters do. It would interfere with their masks. We were in the same room together, but I wouldn't know him if I bumped into him again." There was a bitterness to her voice.

"That's not your fault, Leslie. You had no idea what was going on. No one did."

She nodded her head, but didn't look convinced. "I know that's true. Everything about him looked legit, down to his gear. The only thing that didn't add up was the fact that there was no name on his jacket. If it weren't for that, it looked exactly like the gear every station in the Destiny Fire Department uses."

"Okay, walk me through what happened from the moment you guys first saw him, what he said, and what happened before he ran away."

He listened intently as she told him about seeing the shooter motion for them to follow him. They'd originally thought it was Keyes or Cho needing help. Even when they didn't speak on the radio, Leslie had momentarily wondered if they were having trouble with communications.

Clint could imagine her shock when she rounded the corner to find the mystery firefighter standing there, gun aimed at them.

"Danny tried to talk him down. Suggested we get out of the building and talk. But it didn't make a difference." She wrapped her arms around herself again.

Clint wished he had a jacket or a blanket to offer her, even though he knew the chill she felt was beyond physical cold. He waited patiently for her to continue.

She took in a slow breath. "The guy said that it was too late. That's when he shot Danny."

Chapter Three

She'd lived through the ordeal, and even though she was telling Clint everything, it still didn't seem real. It was as though Leslie was trapped in a strange dream—the kind induced by a high fever—and she couldn't snap out of it. All she wanted to do was wake up and find herself in her bunk at the fire station with Danny's laughter filtering in from the dining area.

"Can you remember exactly what he said? The words he used?"

Leslie nodded. "He told Danny, 'No. It's too late for that.' And that's when he pulled the trigger." She swallowed hard. "I don't understand why any of this happened."

"Did you or Danny approach him at all?"

"No. Danny had both of his hands up, trying to show that we weren't a threat." And she'd been rooted to the floor. Leslie knew there was nothing she could've done to prevent the chain of events, but she wondered if she'd tried to speak if she might have been able to dissuade the shooter. Even as the thought flitted through her mind, she knew the answer.

"Did he ever aim the gun at you?"

"I'm not sure. Danny moved to stand between me and the gun... After that, it was aimed squarely at Danny the entire time." She felt the familiar sting of tears behind her eyelids and tried her best to blink them away. Crying right now would serve no purpose except to give her an even worse headache than the one she was already dealing with.

"After the gun was fired, what did the suspect do?"

"He immediately turned and left the room." She closed her eyes and let the scene play again in her mind. "He didn't run, and he never looked back. He walked out. Like those action movies where someone throws a grenade into a building and walks away like it's no big deal as the explosion goes off behind him."

When she opened her eyes again, she half expected Clint to be looking at her as though she might be going crazy. Instead, his gaze was filled with a combination of respect and determination.

Maybe she and Clint weren't close friends, but she'd know him long enough to trust he would do everything in his power to find the man who'd tried to kill Danny. She just wished she had a description or something to help. Because if he did manage to get out of the warehouse alive and undetected, once he dumped the gear, it'd be nearly impossible to find him.

Clint must've been thinking along the same lines. "If you heard the man's voice again, would you recognize it?"

She wished there'd been something distinctive about the shooter's voice. "I don't think so." The idea that, if this guy managed to escape the warehouse and make it past everyone outside, he might get away with it all made her stomach ache. "I keep going over it in my head, and none of this makes sense. There had to be something else we could do. But we never thought something like this could happen."

Leslie wanted some answers. Becca would need them when she arrived in Destiny. Right now, they had nothing.

A touch to her hand brought Clint's face into focus.

He watched her with concern. "No one could've predicted that an armed assailant might be hiding inside a burning warehouse." His phone rang, and he gave her hand a gentle squeeze before standing up and answering it. "Baker here."

Leslie slid her hands between her thighs and the chair she was sitting on. She jiggled her right foot up and down as she watched Clint. Had someone found the shooter? She really needed some good news. When Becca arrived at the hospital, Leslie wanted to be able to tell her that the man who shot her husband was in custody.

For the tenth time, she lifted a silent prayer that Danny would be okay.

Clint listened intently for several moments before relaying what Leslie had said about the man in the ware-house. "I agree. Having someone posted outside Bracken's room once he's out of surgery would be a good idea." He glanced at Leslie, but his expression was unreadable. "Understood. I'll call once we get an update."

He slipped the phone back into his pocket and sat down on the chair next to hers. "That was a detective I work with. The fire's out, although it'll be a while before the inspector can go in and officially determine what started it."

There was something in his voice that told Leslie there was more to the story. They always had to have an official investigation done when it came to fires, especially if insur-ance was involved. Often, though, the cause of the fire was obvious. "But Holden or Warren had a guess."

Clint nodded once. "Kerosene was used as an accelerant."

"There'd be no need for kerosene in a warehouse like that. Especially one that's specifically storing paper."

"Exactly. The inspector will check into it further as soon as it's safe to do so. In the meantime, there are security cameras for that warehouse as well as other warehouses in the same vicinity. We'll be combing through the footage to see if we can catch a glimpse of the arsonist. And the shooter, assuming they're two different individuals."

Nausea swirled in Leslie's stomach. "Which means he hasn't been caught yet."

"There's been so sign of him. We're searching the warehouse, but it's expansive with aisles of boxes filled with paper waiting for distribution. There are countless places to hide. He also could've slipped out in the chaos before additional units even arrived."

A nightmare. This whole thing was a complete nightmare.

What if Danny didn't make it? What if the shooter got away with this? The idea that he could just be out there somewhere made Leslie nervous. She homed in on what Clint said regarding someone being posted outside Danny's room.

"Do you think someone might come here to hurt Danny?"

Clint studied her face for a moment. "Honestly? I don't know. But we'd rather take precautions. The truth is, there's more to the situation than we know right now. If you and Bracken had stumbled on some kind of crime in progress, then our suspect wouldn't have been wearing firefighter gear. Whatever was going on, it was thought out. Planned way in advance."

"Which means there was probably an escape route planned, too."

"Agreed. Even if the person who shot Bracken was responsible for setting the warehouse fire in the first place, wearing the gear suggests he had no intention of dying in there."

Leslie was in desperate need of some caffeine. Something to give her a little jolt of energy and maybe... just maybe... clear her head. But she didn't see any in the immediate vicinity, and she didn't want to leave if Becca arrived or the doctor came out with an update. "There are way too many possibilities. Too many unknowns."

"Agreed. I think Detective Paris is taking the case. We'll systematically go through everything and see if we can piece together what happened. For now, we'll wait for word on Bracken. Hopefully the doctor will be able to recover the bullet, which we can run through ballistics and look for a match."

"Right. We wait." She hated waiting. Didn't everybody, though? Was Clint going to stay with her? The way he worded it made it sound like he was.

Now that the fire was out, other members of their company would be arriving at the hospital as soon as they could. Until then, the last thing she wanted was to sit alone. It was too easy to let her thoughts wander. To think of all the what-ifs. Or the things she might have done to change the outcome.

"Can I get you something to drink? Or eat?"

Clint's concerned voice broke through her thoughts.

"What? Oh." She glanced at the nurse's station where everything was just as it had been minutes earlier. "Yeah. I need something caffeinated. Coffee. Or a Coke."

"I'll be right back." He stood, lightly touched her shoulder, and left the waiting area.

Leslie's phone rang, and her sister's name popped up on the screen. She took a steady breath and answered it. "Hey, Cindy. Is everything okay?"

Immediately, Leslie heard the cries of her two-year-old niece, Bree, in the background.

"Oh, it's great." Her voice was thick with sarcasm. "Bree has another double ear infection, and she's just a mess. I'm waiting for the pharmacy to fill her antibiotic, but the doctor said it'll take at least twenty-four hours before she starts feeling better. Once she starts the meds." Cindy paused. "The doctor is going to refer us to an ENT and is recommending they put tubes in her ears."

Poor baby. Bree had dealt with far more than her fair share of ear infections in her two years of life. If tubes would finally end the constant cycle of infections and antibiotics, it would be worth it.

Cindy, her husband Peter, and their two girls lived in Destiny less than fifteen minutes from Leslie's house. She saw them often. Right now, five-year-old Izzy was obsessed with talking to Leslie on the phone. Sometimes the conversations the girl started had Leslie in stitches.

"I'm sorry you're going through all of this. I hope, if the ENT agrees that tubes are necessary, that they'll help Bree feel better. She's had more than her fair share of ear infection."

"She sure has. I just hope Peter can be here for the procedure."

Peter had been traveling out of town for work since before the girls were born. It was getting harder and harder on Cindy now, though. Especially when Bree was sick.

"Let me know when you find out about the procedure. I'll arrange for vacation and come take care of Izzy."

Cindy's sigh of relief was palpable even over the phone. "Thank you. I appreciate that."

"Anytime."

"I'm hoping the ENT will call back with an appointment. Peter should be home by dinner tonight. I'll talk to him about it then, too." There was shuffling in the background. Bree's cries were closer, but they were starting to calm a little.

An announcement went over the hospital's loudspeakers and must have carried over the phone call.

"Where are you?"

"I'm at the hospital. Danny was hurt today. He's in surgery." Leslie didn't want to elaborate. Not right now.

"Les. I'm sorry. Is he going to be okay?"

"I don't know yet. I'm hoping they'll come out to give us an update soon. Prayers are appreciated." Movement caught her eye. She lifted her chin to find Clint approaching, a large cup of coffee in his right hand, and a paper bag in his left. He gave her a questioning look. "Hey, I've got to go. I'll call you later, okay?"

"Yeah. Okay. Love ya."

"Love you, too." Leslie ended the call and cradled the phone in the palm of her hand. She suppressed a sigh as everything over the last couple of hours shifted like an unsteady weight on her shoulders. How was she going to balance it all without something falling out of place?

Clint reclaimed his chair. "Any news?"

"No, that was my sister. My niece is sick, and my sister is kinda running on empty right now, trying to take care of everything by herself."

"I'm sorry to hear that." He handed over the coffee. "I

don't know how you like it, so I came prepared." He opened the paper bag and proceeded to pull out a variety of single-use packets of sugar and creamer cups. "Hopefully something in here will work."

Leslie chose two packets of raw sugar and two cups of vanilla creamer. "This is amazing. Thank you." She took the lid off the cup, added everything, and stirred it. As soon as she replaced the lid, she took a sip and imagined the warm liquid permeating every cell in her body.

When she looked over at him, she found him watching her. The corners of his mouth twitched with amusement.

"I know. I should have a little coffee with my sugar and cream." Her sister was always criticizing Leslie for the amount of "stuff" she put in her coffee.

"Oh, no judgement here. I imagine I'd have to put twice that to make it palatable for me."

"You don't like coffee?"

He gave his head a decisive shake. "I love the smell of it but can't stand the taste."

"Truthfully? I prefer a good cup of hot chocolate or chocolate milk any day. But beggars can't be choosers." Leslie took another sip. Honestly, it was some pretty terrible coffee that was barely made palatable with all the sugar and creamer that she'd added. That's why she typically went with a bottle of Coke if she needed the caffeine. At least she knew what it was going to taste like every time.

"I don't know about that." He reached into the bag and produced a large chocolate chip cookie wrapped in plastic. "I didn't know if you were hungry but figured few people can turn down chocolate."

The cookie was nearly as big as her hand. She was about to suggest they split it when a nurse walked toward them from across the room.

Leslie set the cookie down on the chair and stood, her hands cupped around her coffee. Clint stood with her.

The nurse, whose name tag read Humphrey, extended a hand to Clint. "The doctor removed a single bullet from Daniel Bracken's chest. He said you'd want it for evidence right away."

"Yes, thank you." Clint lifted the jar and looked inside. "I'll get this to the lab right away."

"How's Danny doing?" Somehow, Leslie's voice sounded calm. Normal. Not at all representative of how she felt on the inside.

"The doctor is working on him now. The bullet missed his heart, but there was extensive damage. He'll come out and give you an update once he's wrapped up the surgery." The nurse reached over and laid a hand on Leslie's shoulder. "I'm sorry I don't have more information for you."

"I understand. Thank you."

The nurse crossed the room and disappeared behind a set of double doors. Only then did Leslie allow herself to drop into her chair.

Nurse Humphrey hadn't said much, but it sounded like Danny's condition wasn't good. She prayed for guidance and steady hands for the surgeon, that Becca would arrive as quickly as possible, and that the bullet might give the police a lead toward finding Danny's shooter.

Chapter Four

Clint hated leaving Leslie at the hospital, but several members of her company had arrived to offer support to Danny while they waited for word on his condition. Apparently, Danny's wife was back in town and on her way to the hospital. Leslie had people there to support her now. The best thing Clint could do was get the bullet to the station and see if they could match it to another crime in the area.

As soon as he dropped it off at the lab, he swung by Detective John Paris's office. John was leading the investigation into the shooting as well as the warehouse fire.

He found the detective on the phone but was quickly waved inside. Clint closed the door behind him and took a seat across the desk. He checked the texts on his phone while he waited for John to finish his conversation.

"I checked on him at lunch and will go back to the house for a while around dinner. I'm glad your mom is doing better. Eve, honey, I've got to run. I'll talk to you soon. Give everyone my love... I love you, too." John ended the call and put his cell phone down on the desk. "Sorry about that. Eve's mom had surgery yesterday, so Eve went down to help for a few days."

Eve and John were married over a year ago. She worked as the chief medical examiner at the morgue in the same building as the police department. The couple were well known and liked by everyone at the precinct.

"I hope her mom recovers quickly."

"Thank you. The surgery is fairly minor but will impair Gemma's mobility for a couple of weeks. Eve wanted to stay and help her parents for a few days until they find a new normal." John picked up a pencil and pointed to the photograph of a Yorkie puppy. "I think Eve was more worried about leaving Cody than she was about me." He chuckled.

The couple adopted the puppy a couple of months ago. He was growing like a weed, and at four-months-old, was full of energy. Eve usually brought him into work with her, having constructed a large play area of sorts in her office. Unfortunately, John didn't have a place for her in his and was in and out far too often to bring Cody to the station.

"I'm sure he'll be glad when things return to normal, too."

John nodded, but his expression grew serious. "How's Leslie Granger doing? Did you get an update on Bracken?"

"When I left, he was still in surgery. I was given the bullet recovered from his wound and took that by the lab. Other members of their company are at the hospital now, so Granger isn't alone." Clint intended to check in on all of them again before he went home for the night.

"That's good. We're all praying for Bracken's recovery."

"Any progress on the case? Was the other person missing at the warehouse ever located?"

John sat up straighter in his chair. "Yes. It turns out Sarah never showed up to work. She woke up this morning with symptoms of the flu. She'd called in sick, but the person she spoke with left early, so news of her absence never made its way around the office."

Thank goodness she hadn't been trapped in the fire. As far as the blaze itself went, no one was injured.

"And still no sign of the shooter?"

"None. We have two patrols stationed at the warehouse tonight so, if he is hiding inside, they'll see him when he exits. We'll do a more thorough search once we're cleared to enter the building."

Clint prayed they'd catch him. The fact was, it would be easy to get out and slip away undetected at this point. Especially if he'd had some kind of escape plan in place all along.

"Granger said the suspect told Bracken it was too late to end the confrontation. I just wish we knew whether he said that because Granger and Bracken had interrupted him, or if he was there specifically to target a firefighter."

"If it was the latter, then it begs the questions—was our suspect determined to shoot just any firefighter, or was Bracken the target?" John dropped the pencil he was holding eraser-first onto the top of his desk. He snatched it out of the air when it bounced back up again. "We'll have an officer stationed at the hospital for the time being. If he was the intended target, then the suspect may go back to finish the job. I'm looking into the warehouse and paper plant in general. I want to know if there are any outstanding disputes with current or past employees, contracts, or even competitors. See if there's a reason why someone would be targeting the company as a whole."

"What can I do?"

"Since you know Granger, why don't you talk to her as well as others at the fire station. Find out if they've had any issues recently. If any of their people have had run-ins with someone during their call outs that made responding to fires difficult for any reason. Talk to Bracken's wife. See if there's anyone he's had a confrontation with outside of work."

"You've got it. I'll see if we can track down the equipment the suspect was wearing. It sounds like it looked exactly like everyone else's minus the name tag. If we can figure out where he got it, maybe it'll lead us to an ID."

"That sounds like a plan to me. Let me know if you find anything."

"Will do."

The sooner they connected the dots, the better. Until they found the suspect and got him off the streets, Clint was going to worry about the safety of Leslie and everyone else at the station.

"We haven't had any trouble—certainly nothing recent." Fire Chief Menendez poured a cup of coffee and offered it to Clint. When the officer politely declined, Menendez kept it for himself and led the way to his office. "There's the occasional case of arson where our inspectors discover proof leading to the arrest of the person responsible. But even then, we don't usually see a lot of backlash."

That was certainly true. Destiny's fire department and police department often worked hand-in-hand. While most firefighters were seen as the heroes they were, that wasn't always the case with officers. Clint had personally come face-to-face with people who were angry at him for interrupting a dispute or arresting a loved one.

He always sought to do what he could to serve the town

of Destiny and improve the lives of the people who lived there. Some days were easier than others.

"You've never had one of your firefighters singled out? Either in a negative or a positive light?"

"Well, sure. It happens on occasion. Cho carried a baby out of a burning building last week and was on the front page of the newspaper. Last month, Keyes stumbled on the evidence of an arson-based fire that led to an arrest."

"Could you put together a list for me with any instances that stand out over the last four to six months?"

"Absolutely. The station is at your disposal. We all want the shooter caught as soon as possible." Chief Menendez glanced at his cell phone which was lying face up on the desk between them. "I keep hoping someone at the hospital will call with some good news. I want to be there myself while they wait, but someone still needs to manage the station. We've got a company that's filling in for Bracken's so his can wait with Granger. Once Bracken is out of surgery and in recovery, I'll head that way."

Clint could imagine everyone from Station #2 would be there if they could. That would be the case if someone from the precinct were in the hospital for a similar reason.

"I can understand that." Clint checked his notes. "We're in the preliminary stages of this investigation. I hate to ask this, but was Bracken having any trouble in his personal life? Was there anyone he didn't get along with outside of the station?"

Menendez leaned back in his chair and immediately shook his head. "Not that I know of. He was well liked. A bit of a class clown, if you know what I mean. Quick to tease the others, but always in a good-natured way. If he was having any difficulties, he never shared that with me. If anyone might know, though, it'd be Granger."

The chief looked at his phone again and shifted his weight. It was clear he was ready to check in with his people and do something more than just sit there. Clint could certainly empathize.

"I have one more question, then I'll get out of your way. Granger said the shooter wore gear that was identical to what you all wear, except there was no name on the jacket. How do you get your gear? Is something like that easy to get a hold of for anyone who doesn't work for the fire department?"

"The fire department purchases gear from several different suppliers depending on which is offering the most competitive price at the time. We have strict policies in place when it comes to what we purchase and what it's for. While some of our firefighters might purchase smaller accessory items according to their personal preference, essential personal protective equipment is provided. Each firefighter is responsible for the upkeep of their equipment. So, no, someone wouldn't be able to easily purchase a full set of gear like that. But commandeer a set from one of our stations?" Menendez frowned. "As much as I hate to admit it, it's not outside the realm of possibility."

"I know this station is brand new. Has everything been moved over, or are there still some things waiting to be transferred?"

"Everything's here, and we double and triple checked the inventory." The chief looked thoughtful. "We have eight fire stations in town. I'll reach out and make sure each one goes through their gear—ours included."

"That sounds like a good plan. In the meantime, we're investigating things from the warehouse side. We've also got people keeping an eye on Bracken at the hospital, just in case he really was the target." Clint pushed away from the desk and stood. "I'd like for us to keep in touch. If you find out anything, please call me or contact Detective Paris at the precinct. I'll be sure to keep you updated on everything as well."

"Absolutely." Menendez stood as well and reached out to shake hands. "We appreciate the way the PD has teamed up with us on this."

Clint gave the chief's hand a hearty shake. "We wouldn't have it any other way."

Before he could turn to leave, Menendez's cell phone rang. He held up a finger to stop Clint's exit. "This is Menendez." There were several moments of silence as he listened to whoever was talking on the other end of the line. "That's good news. Yes, I will." He focused on Clint, relief on his face. "Bracken made it through the surgery. The bullet narrowly missed his heart. The next few days may be tough, but barring any difficulties, he should make a full recovery."

Clint's shoulders relaxed as he took in the news. "I'm glad to hear that. I'll be praying his stay in the hospital is a short one."

"Thank you."

As he walked through the fire station and into the cool November air, he thought about his conversation with the chief. There were several personal questions about Danny that he wanted to ask Leslie once he got back to the hospital. With any luck, maybe Danny would be feeling well enough to answer a few questions himself tomorrow.

Chapter Five

The last of the sun sank below the horizon, turning the hospital parking lot into an eerie expanse dotted with vehicles and lit by yellow-tinged streetlights overhead. It wasn't even seven o'clock. The short days were one of Leslie's biggest complaints about this time of year. Sometimes, when she was home alone, she felt trapped by the darkness. She already missed the long, warm days of summer.

When Officer Baker—Clint—came back to the hospital, he brought a bag of burgers with him. It was a thoughtful gesture, and one everyone from the station appreciated. The food was a welcome distraction as everyone took turns telling Becca funny or encouraging stories about Danny while she waited for the nurse to take her back to see her husband.

Leslie had tried to focus on her delicious burger but barely made it halfway through when she'd finally wrapped it back up and set it aside.

Danny had made it through surgery. Miraculously, the bullet barely missed his heart, but he'd lost a lot of blood, and arterial damage meant repairs had still been extensive. The doctor had warned it might be some time before he was awake and talking. While the doctor felt he would make a full recovery, the risk of infection was still very real.

Becca mostly sat in the chair next to Leslie's, her hand resting on her rounded belly as she talked about their unborn baby and how they were decorating the nursery. They'd chosen a jungle theme since they weren't going to find out the gender until he or she was born.

When the nurse finally allowed her to go back and see her husband, Becca hurriedly followed. Leslie hadn't seen her since.

With the exception of allowing the chief in to see Danny when he stopped by, everyone else was informed that they'd be welcome to see him during visiting hours the following day.

Everyone who was still on shift got ready to head back to the station. Bryce offered to take Leslie's gear back with him, which she appreciated.

The chief, however, insisted that Leslie take the rest of her shift off to get some extra sleep. She appreciated his concern, but she really wasn't looking forward to going home to her empty house where she knew she'd be dreaming about the fire and shooting once she went to bed.

"I understand the need to keep yourself busy, but I'm going to have to insist. Danny's still alive because you worked quickly to get him out of that warehouse. You deserve to get some rest." Chief Menendez rested a hand on her shoulder. "Besides, I think Officer Baker had a few more questions for you." He tilted his head toward Clint, who had stuck around all evening and was currently leaning against a chair nearby.

He stood and approached. "I'd be happy to give you a

ride back to the station so you can pick up your vehicle. I promise the questions won't take long."

"Sure. That would be great. Thank you." Leslie focused on her boss. "Please keep me in the loop, sir. And if you need me back in, just call."

"Will do. Go get some sleep."

She would... eventually. "Yes, sir."

Chief Menendez strode purposefully through the waiting area and out a set of double doors.

"What about you? Are you ready to get out of here?"

Leslie glanced at the nurse's station. On one hand, part of her wanted to stay close by in case Becca needed something, or to hear if there was a change in Danny's condition. The truth was, though, Becca had her contact information. The hospital promised to keep the chief updated. There was nothing else for Leslie to do. "I thought you had a few more questions."

"I can ask them in the car on the way back to the station. I figured we can multi-task." His expression was open with an underlying concern.

Was he worried about her emotional or mental status? Or did she look as worn out as she felt? Even if she wasn't ready to sleep, she could definitely use a shower to wash the day away. Before heading home, though, she might take a quick detour into the station and grab a piece of that chocolate cream pie before everyone else ate it all.

Minutes later, she was in the passenger seat of his squad car. "For the record, this is my first time in a police car."

Clint chuckled and glanced at her as he pulled out of the hospital parking lot. "Good to know. So you didn't leave behind a life of crime to become a firefighter?"

She laughed at that. "I considered the exciting life of a career criminal but decided to go a different route. Fighting fires brings that exhilaration, camaraderie, and the chance to help others without risk of jail time."

"Then I'd say you made a wise choice."

"I'd like to think so."

Clint drove the dark streets to the loop that would take them around to the south side of town. "I'm sure your family is proud of you."

"I appreciate that. My mom passed away eight years ago from cancer. I'd just decided to pursue this as a career, and she was really excited for me. Dad was supportive, too. He passed away two years later. It's just me and my older sister now. I know she's proud of me in general, but she thinks I should've chosen something less dangerous with a more regular schedule." She paused, uncertain how much to share. She'd known Clint for a couple of years, but they'd never just chatted about family or interests.

"I'm sorry to hear about your parents." His voice was quiet. "I can only imagine how hard that must've been. I'm sorry your sister isn't more supportive. Does she live in Destiny?"

Leslie wasn't sure if it was the exhaustion of the day or because Clint had been there helping them ever since the warehouse, but her reluctance to share more than necessary melted away. "Thank you. Yes, Cindy lives here. She's... well, she hasn't had it easy. Her youngest daughter is sick all the time, and her husband is away on business six out of seven days of the week. Sometimes more than that. I know she's overwhelmed, and it's hard when I can't always help because of my work schedule."

There was a lot more to it than that. Cindy chose to be a stay-at-home mom when Izzy was born, but Leslie wasn't so sure that it was what Cindy really wanted to do even though she was an amazing mom and great with the girls.

"I'm sure that's stressful and piles on guilt that you don't necessarily need to carry." Clint was silent as they pulled up to Station #2 and parked. He turned to look at her, his brown eyes filled with compassion. "I'll be keeping both you and your sister in my prayers."

She blinked in surprise as his words settled over her heart like a soothing balm. "That's really kind. I appreciate that." The station's lights brightened the parking lot. "What about you? Do you have family in the area?"

"I do. My parents and a younger brother named Drew. We moved here right before I started high school. My parents figured we'd stay here for a year or two, but we ended up loving the community and never left. Most of our extended family is in Wyoming, so we travel that way on a semi-regular basis."

"That sounds nice." Leslie glanced at the clock, surprised that it was nearing nine. "You said you wanted to ask me some questions before we left the hospital. I have a hard time believing you meant talking about my family's drama."

He chuckled then and ran a hand over his neatly trimmed mustache and beard. "Maybe not, but it was a bonus." For just a moment, he smiled at her and seemed to truly mean what he said before shifting into a more serious mood. "Was there anything going on in Danny's life that he was worried about? Financial issues, problems in his marriage, or someone he had a conflict with? Chief Menendez suggested that, since you and he spend a lot of time training together, that you would be the person to ask."

Leslie tried to school her surprise at that but had a feeling she'd failed. "He and Becca are great. The two of them have always been cute together. Danny's so excited about the baby. They've been planning the nursery and collecting names to choose from once the baby's born."

She went back over the conversations she'd had with Danny in the last few weeks. She hadn't thought about it before, but most of them were relatively superficial. "We mostly talk about work, movies or television, and the baby. I don't think he's ever uttered a word about finances, the rest of his family, or anyone he might've had issues with."

Then again, she didn't share a lot about her family issues with him, either. What did that say about their working relationship? Probably nothing except it's just the way it worked.

Clint studied her for a moment before giving a single nod. "Thank you. We're trying to look at all angles of this." He pulled his wallet out and handed her a business card. "If you think of anything else, or if you need something, please don't hesitate to call me."

Their fingers brushed as she took it from him. "I appreciate it. Thanks again for the drive back to the station."

"Not a problem. You heading home?"

"As soon as I grab a few things from my locker."

"All right. Be safe, Leslie."

"Thanks. You, too." She got out of the squad car and gave him a wave before walking to the station.

Twenty minutes later, her gear was stored away, her backpack in the passenger seat of her car, and two slices of chocolate cream pie were sitting on a paper plate on the floorboard.

She stifled a yawn as she drove home through the dark streets. It was early enough in the night for there to still be plenty of cars on the road but late enough it wasn't busy.

As much as she'd hated it when the chief insisted she take the rest of her shift off, Leslie was thankful when she pulled into the driveway of her small two-bedroom house and knew that her bed was waiting for her inside. It was a blessing in disguise because maybe she could get some sleep before she needed to take Dad to his appointment. She'd go to bed—after she ate a piece of chocolate cream pie, of course.

With the strap of her backpack over one shoulder and the pie balanced on one hand, she shut the car door and used the fob to lock it. She fumbled with the keys as she approached the front door.

She reached up to slip the key into the doorknob and stopped.

A sliver of light peeked out between the door and the frame. Instead of being closed and locked securely like she'd left it, the door was open just enough to let out a little of the light inside.

Leslie's heart stalled then started to thump wildly in her chest. Everything was quiet, but she couldn't shake the feeling that someone was inside just waiting for her to push that door open. She retreated back to the car, tossed her backpack inside and the pie onto the seat, then got in herself and locked the door.

She dug her wallet from the front pocket of her backpack and took out the business card that Clint had given her. Her hands shook as she dialed his number.

Chapter Six

On his way back to the precinct, Clint had gone through a drive through for a soda. He wanted to stick around the station and see how the investigation was going and knew he'd need a sugar pick-me-up. He'd just pulled into the police station's parking lot and was getting out of his car when his phone rang. He didn't hesitate to answer even though it showed it was from an unknown caller. He handed out business cards to a lot of people he didn't know.

"This is Officer Clint Baker."

"Clint? It's Leslie."

She was about the last person he expected to hear from, especially considering he'd just seen her half an hour ago. The urgent tone to her voice had him instantly on alert.

"Leslie? What's wrong?"

"I just got home, and the front door isn't latched shut. I always, *always* lock the door behind me when I leave."

"What's your address?" He got back into his car and rushed to put his seatbelt on.

She told him, and he entered it into his GPS.

"I'm on my way. Is it possible your sister might have gone in for something and forgot to close the door?"

"No. At least, I can't imagine she would have. She has a key, but she's never used it, not without telling me."

"Don't enter the house until I get there. I'm only three minutes away." He didn't realize she lived so close and sent up a silent prayer of thanks that was the case.

If someone had broken into her place, the last thing he wanted was for her to unwillingly step into the middle of things and get hurt. Or worse.

"I went back to my car and locked the door. No one's come out of the house, and I don't see any shadows moving inside."

"Good thinking. Just let me know if you see any movement. Whatever you do, don't leave the car until I get there. I need to call this in." He kept her on the line and used his radio to speak to dispatch. "This is unit seven. Show me responding to a possible residential break-in." He gave the address. "I'm en route now, with an ETA of less than three minutes."

"Understood, unit seven. Sending an additional unit to meet you there."

"Copy that." He returned his focus to his phone call with Leslie. "I'm approaching your house now." He'd chosen to make a silent approach as he turned onto her street. He didn't want to spook anyone who might still be inside the house. He parked right behind her car then got out and strode to her driver's side window. She rolled it down. "Backup will be here in a minute. We'll go inside and clear the house. Once we've done that, you can come inside and see if anything's missing."

"Yeah. Okay." She looked over at her house then back with a nod. Worry had created small creases near the corners of her mouth and deepened the lines between her brows.

Clint hated that she was going through this. Especially after everything else she'd dealt with today.

The second police vehicle to arrive was a Suburban, and Clint knew immediately that it was Officer Gabe Harrison and his K-9 partner, Loki. Even better. If someone was hiding in the house, they wouldn't stay hidden long with the talented dog on the scene.

Clint rested his hand on her shoulder. "I'll be back as soon as I can."

"Please be careful."

He waited long enough to see that she'd rolled her window back up before jogging to where Gabe was preparing Loki. The dog barely registered Clint's presence as he focused on his trainer and friend. Once Loki had on the correct collar and lead, Gabe allowed him to exit the kennel in the back of the vehicle.

Together, the three of them approached the front of the house. It was a single-story building, which would make it easier to search. Just like Leslie had told him, the door was open just enough to see the light from inside. Cautiously, Clint pushed it open with his foot.

Gabe raised his voice as he spoke, "This is the Destiny Police Department. We're coming in with a K-9 officer. If there's anyone in here, I need you to announce your presence for your safety."

Silence.

Clint led the way into the house with Gabe on his six. One-by-one, they searched each room, closets included, until both officers were satisfied that no one was inside.

Gabe got a ball out and tossed it to Loki, praising him for a job well done. He patted the dog's rump. "There was glass on the floor of the second bedroom right beneath the window. I bet that's how they gained access. If it weren't for that and the open door, I never would've known someone broke in."

"Agreed." Clint went back to inspect the front door. "I'm going to take a closer look at that window and the back door."

The back door was still locked. So were all the windows for the one in the second bedroom. His boot crunched on the broken bits of glass beneath the open window. He moved the curtains aside with his flashlight to reveal a hole in the bottom pane. No doubt someone had busted the hole and reached through to unlock the window.

He made his way back to the living room where Gabe and Loki were waiting.

"Looks like you were right. The intruder came in through the spare bedroom window and must have left through the front door."

Gabe frowned. "Well, if anything was stolen, it's not obvious. The TV and DVD players are still here. I'm pretty sure I noticed a laptop in the bedroom. Nothing looks disturbed or damaged."

They reached out to dispatch and gave an update on the situation and requested a forensics team.

Clint jabbed a thumb at the front door. "I'm going to let Leslie know and have her come in and look around. We'll need forensics for that window. See if there are any finger-prints left behind. Same with the front door."

"Sounds like a plan. If you're good here, Loki and I will get back out on patrol."

"Yep. Thanks, man." They shook hands and Clint gave Loki's ear a rub.

Outside, the streetlight cast just enough of a glow on Leslie's car to illuminate her face. She rolled the window down as he approached.

"You did the right thing calling. Someone did break into your house. They were likely long gone before you got home." He hated the look of fear that flashed across her face. Her home was supposed to be her safe space, and it'd been violated. It was likely a random hit, but he knew she'd be worried about it until the intruder was caught. "Aside from the window they broke to gain entry, nothing else looks like it's destroyed or obviously missing. If you're up to it, it'd be helpful if you came inside and had a look around."

"Yeah. Of course." She followed him inside, her arms crossed tightly across her chest as though she were cold.

It was the beginning of November, and the evenings were finally starting to cool off after an unusually hot summer. No doubt that contributed to the chill Leslie was experiencing, but most of her response was likely related to the events of the day. The poor woman had to be exhausted after everything she'd been through.

"Go through the house, check any hidden valuables you might have as well, and let me know if there's anything missing or out of place."

She gave a distracted nod, her attention already on her surroundings. As much as Clint wanted to stay close by in case she needed anything, he waited in the living room to give her space.

While she was looking around, it gave him a chance to really take in the look and feel of the house. It wasn't fancy, but the simple style resulted in a place that was comfortable. Welcoming. Colors were pretty neutral, but it was clear her favorite color was a light purple because accent pillows, candles, and pictures all sported the same shade.

The most impressive area of the house, however, was the far side of the living room. The wall was lined with bookcases except for the very center where an oversized accent chair and matching ottoman sat. It was the perfect reading nook. He imagined Leslie curled up there well into the night with the floor lamp nearby casting just enough light to read by.

Along with more books than he could count, there was also an extensive Funko Pop! figure collection. They were organized by sets or type and set up between or in front of books, whichever seemed to fit the best.

The cast from Lord of the Rings was arranged together on one side of a shelf next to the books while characters from the show Friends were set up in another location. A shelf with adventure books held many of the cartoon characters from Disney's Robin Hood movie. After glancing at the entire collection, there wasn't a single figure that Clint didn't recognize.

"I know. I've got a bit of an addiction." Leslie's soft voice, tinged with humor, came from his left. "In my defense, I've been collecting them for years. I'm still looking for Robin Hood to finish that set." She pointed to the empty spot between Maid Marian and Little John. "I'll find it one of these days."

"I think it's awesome. I only have three, and all given to me by my brother. One of them looks like me dressed as a cop." He chuckled. "Then I've got a Batman and Robin duo. I like them, but there are so many. I guess I had a hard time narrowing down my choices."

"I get that." She slipped her hands into her pockets. "If anything was stolen from the house, it's not obvious. They didn't touch the jewelry or electronics. Or even these." She swept a hand in front of the bookcase before burying it in her pocket again. "I have several that are hard to find and worth something if they went to the trouble of listing them on Ebay."

"I don't know why someone broke into your place. I suspect they went out the front door, and that's why it wasn't closed all the way. I suppose it's possible that they were going to leave that way when you pulled into the driveway forcing them to go back out the window. Maybe they didn't have a chance to go through your house or steal anything before you returned?"

It was a good theory. Once their forensics team arrived, Clint had every intention of knocking on the doors of the homes across the street to see if they'd noticed anything. With any luck, someone would have a doorbell camera pointed this way.

"Yeah. Maybe." She shivered. Her lips parted as though she were going to ask a question, but a moment later, she pressed them together again.

Clint turned to face her. "What is it?"

She continued to hesitate, and a pink flush filled her cheeks. "I know I've watched way too many true crime documentaries, but what if someone broke in here just to set up a camera or microphone? Is there a way to search for something like that? I'd rather seem neurotic than find out later that some perv was watching me."

"That's not neurotic. That's smart. And forensics should have a device we can use to sweep for bugs. If there's anything transmitting a signal, we'll find it."

Her shoulders dropped noticeably with relief. "Thank you."

Clint had responded to plenty of break-ins and

burglaries in the past, and none of them looked like this. Usually, the motives were immediately apparent. That wasn't the case here.

Frustrated, he prayed they'd be able to give Leslie some answers soon.

Chapter Seven

Leslie waited at her kitchen table as officers dusted for fingerprints and did a thorough sweep of her house. Clint waited with her most of the time. Much to her relief, no cameras or listening devices were discovered.

Once the officers had finished gathering evidence and cleared the scene, Clint helped her board up the window until she could have it replaced the next day.

"Could you go and stay with your sister tonight?" Clint glanced at the watch on his wrist.

Leslie checked the time, too. It was well after ten o'clock. "No, I don't want to bother her. My niece has been sick, plus my brother-in-law should've gotten home this evening after being out of town for the last six days. They don't need my drama thrown into the mix."

Besides, as much as she loved her sister, she was afraid they might kill each other if they were forced to stay in the same house for more than a few hours.

"I just hate the idea of you staying here by yourself after

everything that's happened." There was no pity in his eyes, only worry and sincerity.

His concern sent tendrils of warmth straight to her heart. She wasn't used to this. Usually, it was her who was worried about and taking care of everyone else. Or at least it seemed that way. To have someone worried about *her* and wanting to make sure she was taken care of meant a lot.

"I appreciate that, but this house is probably the safest place I could be now. You guys checked every nook and cranny. I'm not going to lie. I even peeked under the beds while you were still here just to be sure." She chuckled at the silliness of it. Still, if she hadn't, she might have worried later when it was just her in the house. "I'll be fine. I'm going to eat a slice of chocolate cream pie that I pilfered from the fire station, batten down the hatches, and try to get some rest. There's no way they're coming back to the same house. Not so soon after an attempted robbery." Or whatever this was.

She thought Clint might argue. Instead, he gave her an exaggerated look of confusion. "Chocolate cream pie? Oh, my grandmother had an amazing recipe for that. She passed away when I was a teen. I think my mom may still have the recipe somewhere."

"I'm sorry to hear about your grandmother. That's neat that she used to bake for you. Would you like a slice? I have two."

"Please don't feel obligated to share your stolen pie."

Now on a mission, she laughed as she hopped up and retrieved the two slices from the fridge along with plates and forks. "I don't mind. I almost felt bad taking two slices, so you'll be alleviating my guilt, anyway." She tossed an amused smile his way.

"Well, I certainly wouldn't want to deprive you of that."

He accepted a piece of pie with a nod of thanks and picked up his fork. He waited for her to sit down before taking a bite. "Okay, that's amazing."

"Right?" Leslie savored the way the mix of sweet and slightly tangy flavors melted on her tongue. Man, she'd needed this. "The guys at the station will tell you I'm obsessed with chocolate." She got up again and took out a can from her fridge. "Especially when you add some whipped cream on top."

When she'd finished adding some to the top of her pie, he reached for the bottle and did the same.

This time, when Leslie took her second bite, she groaned. "Now that's what I'm talking about." She caught him watching her in amusement and felt her cheeks warm. "No making fun of me and my addiction."

"I wouldn't dream of it. Especially when you've been kind enough to share." He was still chuckling when he took another generous bite. "I might have to take a pie the next time I have dinner with my parents. Where did this come from?"

"Kismet Confections. It's just down the street from the station. The owner occasionally brings baked goods in. You should definitely check it out." She claimed that the pies or cakes were leftovers from the day and that she didn't want them to go to waste. Leslie couldn't imagine how an entire chocolate pie survived the day untouched.

"I'll do that. Thank you." He ate the last of his pie and leaned back in his chair with satisfaction. "So you're addicted to chocolate. What's one food or drink you can't stand?"

"Mayonnaise. Anything with mayonnaise." No contest there. She was not a picky person and could eat almost anything put in front of her—unless it had mayonnaise in it. "I know you don't like coffee. What's one food that you can't get enough of?" She used her fork to scrape the last remnants of pie off her plate.

"Lasagna. Or really, anything Italian." He looked thoughtful. "There's a great place on the other side of town. A little restaurant on Maple run by this couple that makes an incredible lasagna. Have you ever been there?"

"No, but I've heard good things about it."

"I'll have to introduce you to it once all of this is wrapped up."

He hadn't quite asked her out on a date, but it was close. Was that his intention? Or was he simply answering her question with an offer to pay her back for sharing the chocolate cream pie?

Feeling suddenly flustered and not sure what to do, she stood and gathered their plates. "You can't go wrong with Italian. It's always nice to find a new place to eat. Some of those smaller restaurants are better than the big chains. They have a personal flair to them."

Leslie carried the plates to the sink. When she turned, Clint was pushing off the small kitchen table to stand. There was no indication that he was encouraged or discouraged by her reply.

"I should probably go and let you get some rest. Please don't be surprised if you see a police car driving up and down the street or even parked outside. We'll increase patrol here at least for tonight until you can get that window fixed and we have time to run fingerprints."

She stood as well. "That sounds good. And it'll make me feel better to know the police are out there, too."

"If this was a run-of-the-mill robbery attempt, chances are they went somewhere else after they came up empty here. With any luck, we'll still have an opportunity to catch them tonight."

"Thanks again for coming. You were the first person I thought to call. You know, since you'd given me your card." Ugh, that wasn't awkward at all. But she was glad he'd given it to her, and she planned to put his contact information in her phone in case she ever needed to call him again.

She'd spent so much time with him the latter half of the day that she was rather sad to see him leave. Even though he was likely ready to get on with his night after everything.

"I'm glad you did. Please don't hesitate to call me again. It doesn't matter what time it is." He ran his fingers through his close-cropped hair. "Would you mind if I checked in on you tomorrow? I'll be sure to keep you updated on the case."

"That would be great." She walked him to the front door.

"Good night, Leslie."

"Good night."

As soon as he left, she closed and locked the door, including the deadbolt. Then she moved a kitchen chair and propped it up under the doorknob. She did the same with the back door.

It took a while to settle down enough to try and sleep. Even then, she left the bedroom and bathroom lights on and curled up on the couch. Between worrying about Danny, replaying the day's events in her head, and then second-guessing Clint's comment about dinner and her awkward response. It wasn't until well after two in the morning before she finally drifted off to sleep.

Even then, she had nightmares of an unknown fire-fighter sneaking into her home in the middle of the night with a gun.

Chapter Eight

The bullet the surgeon removed from Danny Bracken's chest went through ballistics, but there wasn't a match. Clint was hoping it would lead to something. Even if had been matched with a bullet from another unsolved case, at least there would be more evidence to sift through. It might've been enough to lead them in the right direction. Instead, they had nothing.

Detective Paris walked into his office, handed Clint a bottle of water, then took a seat at his desk with his cup of coffee. "Sorry to keep you waiting. I was interviewing a man who worked for the paper company until he was let go a few weeks ago." He took a sip from his cup and leaned back in his chair. "He'd been logging hours he wasn't actually working, got caught, and was officially fired for theft. According to one of the managers, he was quite upset."

"Did it sound like he's the type to burn down the warehouse to get back at the company?"

"I don't think so. He came off as flaky and lazy without the drive to put in the kind of planning and effort our shooter did. He gave me an alibi for the time of the fire. I'll run that down, but I expect it to pan out." Paris set his coffee on the desk. "We went through the security footage taken from any cameras in the vicinity of the warehouse. There was nothing suspicious or unusual. Which makes me think the shooter was familiar with the building and knew how to get inside undetected."

They kept hitting dead ends. The guy hadn't teleported in and out of the building. He had to have gotten inside somehow. "Have you heard when we'll be able to go in and do a thorough search of the warehouse?"

"Not yet. I should find out sometime this afternoon, though. Once we do, we'll take a group of officers in. Only a third of the warehouse was damaged by the flames, so the potential for evidence is high. Especially if the shooter had banked on any evidence being destroyed by the fire." A notification came through on Paris's phone. He checked it then turned the screen off. "Have you gotten anything else on Bracken?"

Clint opened his water and took a swig before twisting the cap back on. "That's the main reason I wanted to stop by. I spoke with Leslie yesterday, and if Bracken was having any difficulties, she said he never talked about it. However, we ran his financials. It turns out he took out a second mortgage on their house less than six months ago. He's also got several credit cards with their limits maxed out. According to their bank account, they've been living paycheck to paycheck for a while."

Hopefully worker's compensation plus insurance would take care of the hospital fees that would add up quickly. Clint doubted Bracken and his wife would be able to handle an astronomical medical bill right now.

"I hate to hear that. But it does mean we need to look into the situation. See if there's anyone Bracken owes money to that doesn't go by the books, if he's received any threats related to money or anything else."

"Agreed. I was planning to go to the hospital and question him after I spoke with you."

Paris nodded his satisfaction and took another drink of his coffee. "How about Leslie Granger? Did you have any luck canvasing her neighborhood?"

"Unfortunately, no." That's what Clint had done for three hours this morning. He knocked on every door that had a view of Leslie's house. No one had video camera footage, and no one noticed anyone strange going in or coming out of the house.

"If it weren't for the fact that the front door had been opened from the inside, I'd think someone broke that back window and ran off." None of it made sense to him. "No fingerprints from the window, so the suspect must have worn gloves. There's a plethora of fingerprints on the front door, but I'm not holding my breath."

"Any other reports of break-ins in the area last night?"

"Two. The first was a vehicle smash and grab two streets over. The other was another home invasion. But in that case, multiple items were stolen and property destroyed. It's possible the suspect was interrupted at Leslie's house and moved on to this one, but so far, we have nothing to connect them."

Clint's gut said they weren't related, but it wasn't like he hadn't been wrong before. Police Chief Dolman said to put extra patrols in the area for the next two nights. Otherwise, they were going to have to treat it like a random event.

"I'd planned to head over to the hospital and have a talk with Bracken. Unless there's another area you want me to focus on."

Paris drained the last of his coffee. "No, that sounds great. Let me know if you find anything out."

"Will do." Clint stood and reached out to shake the other man's hand.

With his half-empty water bottle in hand, he strode to his desk to make a few notes and text Leslie. He'd been thinking about her all morning.

> I hope you got some decent sleep last night. You doing okay?

She didn't know it, but he'd parked just down the street from her house after he'd left her and stayed there several hours before a different officer replaced him so he could get some sleep.

His phone pinged with a reply.

> I got some. I just got to the hospital to visit Danny. Thanks again for your help yesterday.

> No problem. I'm heading that way in just a few minutes.

> Okay. See you in a bit.

He wasn't looking forward to questioning Danny, especially since he and Leslie were friends as well as co-workers. But if there was someone that he'd dealt with that could be targeting him, they needed to know about it.

Clint tried not to think about the worried look on Leslie's face when he'd arrived at the hospital and asked to speak to

Danny alone. She'd encouraged Becca to go with her to the cafeteria to get a snack. Clint promised them he'd just be a few minutes.

Considering Danny had been shot and then revived with CPR while investigating a fire, Clint wasn't sure what to expect. But the man looked better than Clint would've predicted. Still, it was clear Danny was in a great deal of pain, and that was *with* pain medication.

"You look a great deal better than you did when I last saw you." Clint shook the firefighter's hand and sat in the chair that Becca had occupied moments before.

"I heard the nurse gave you guys the bullet. Were you able to get anything from that?" Danny shifted to sit up a little straighter and grimaced.

"I'm afraid not. There was no match to the bullet in the system. We're hoping to get clearance from the fire inspector to go in and thoroughly search the warehouse this afternoon or tomorrow. With any luck, we'll find something to steer us in the right direction."

"I hope so." The blood pressure machine began, and they waited until it had finished getting its reading before Danny spoke again. "You said you had some questions for me."

Starting from the beginning would be a good way to ease into his more difficult questions. "Was there anything about the shooter that seemed familiar? His voice or even how he moved?"

Danny didn't hesitate. "Not even remotely. As far as I know, I'd never seen him before."

"Tell me about the conversation. What did you tell him, and what did he say?"

The firefighter recounted what happened and then gave a description of the man. Everything lined up with Leslie's version of events except that Danny put the shooter at a couple inches taller than her estimate.

"That's great, Danny. We're doing everything we can to find the guy who did this to you." Now it was time for the harder questions before the ladies returned. "Is there anyone you can think of that might want to hurt you? Someone who might've disagreed with how you handle a situation at a call out? What about someone you might owe money to?"

"No one. Why are you asking me that?" Danny's eyes narrowed. "Did you pull my financials?"

"We did. We saw the second mortgage and the credit cards." Clint gave him an apologetic look. He certainly didn't relish getting into the other man's personal business, especially after everything he'd gone through.

When Danny started to pull at the blood pressure cuff, Clint held up his hands. "Look, I'm just trying to help find this guy before he comes after you again, targets your wife, or turns his sights on someone else."

The other man squeezed his eyes closed and let his head rest against the bed for a moment before refocusing on Clint. He leaned forward, his gaze intent. "We do have a lot of debt. It was a combination of poor decisions when we were younger, covering my father-in-law's medical bills, and two rounds of IVF. Am I happy about where we are financially right now? Absolutely not. But it's all above board. I can't think of a single person that would be targeting me or my family."

Danny slumped back against the bed with a groan.

"All right. I'm sorry, but I had to ask." He stood. "We are going to figure out who's behind this. In the meantime, we'll have a police officer posted outside your room. I know Becca's staying here, but we'll keep an eye on your house.

Once you've been released from the hospital, we'll discuss the next steps to keep you and your wife safe."

Danny gave a nod as the door opened. Becca and Leslie stepped back into the room. Becca looked from Clint to her husband and hurried to his side.

"I brought you some pudding and a few snacks." She leaned down and pressed a kiss to his head. "Is everything okay?"

"Officer Baker was assuring me that we'll continue to have an officer nearby until the shooter is caught. I'll fill you in on the rest." He took his wife's hand in his.

Clint pointed at the door. "Let me get out of your hair. Thank you for your time, and I'll be praying for your recovery." He reached over and lightly touched Leslie's arm. "I'll be outside talking to Officer Carrington. Take your time, okay?"

When she nodded her agreement, he left the room.

There was no reason for Clint not to believe Danny. The firefighter seemed genuine. Unfortunately, the lack of any new information meant they weren't any closer to finding the shooter than they were yesterday.

Chapter Nine

Leslie told a story about something Izzy told her on the phone and Danny chuckled. The scowl on his face and the way he clutched at his chest showed instant regret. "I can't laugh right now. There may be a ban on laughing for the next week."

Becca placed a hand over his and gave it a squeeze. The smile on her face didn't quite erase the worry in her eyes, and neither of them came close to the love that shone in every action as she cared for her husband.

"I thought laughter was the best medicine," Leslie teased. "Seriously, though, it's been great to see you awake and talking."

All were good signs. However, it was impossible not to worry about the fact that he was far more pale than normal, and his eyes were dull from pain and medication. It was also clear that the visit from Clint had worn her friend out. She wanted to know what they'd spoken about but didn't want to make him or Becca uncomfortable or any more stressed by asking. They'd share if they wanted to.

"The food here isn't too bad, but if you need any contraband, just say the word." Leslie held up her purse to show them she had plenty of room to sneak something in. "We'll try to hold down the fort until you get back."

The doctor had checked on Danny that morning and said they wanted to keep him for at least a couple more days to make sure everything was healing the way it was supposed to.

The guys from the fire station had already set up a visiting schedule to keep Danny company and give Becca a break so she could go home and take a shower or get some sleep.

Danny's hospital room was filled with balloons and flowers. Someone had even found a balloon of a fire engine which made Leslie chuckle.

A nurse pushed a cart in, adjusted Danny's blood pressure cuff, and typed something into the computer. "Mr. Bracken, physical therapy will be here in about five minutes to help you try to stand. The more we can get you moving, the easier it'll be to heal." She rolled her cart back out into the hallway and closed the door behind her.

"I should probably go, too." Leslie stood from the small hospital chair she'd been perched in. Besides, it'd already been twenty minutes since Clint left. He'd wanted to speak with her, and she didn't want to keep him waiting too long.

Danny glanced at the door to make sure no one else was coming in and they were the only three in the room. "Promise to call me or Becca if you hear anything?"

"Of course. You just concentrate on resting and feeling better, okay?

Leslie sent a silent prayer heavenward that Danny would continue to stay strong as his body healed.

Outside of the room, she found Clint and Officer Carrington talking. She waited awkwardly for them to finish. When Officer Carrington left with a polite wave, Clint turned to her with a smile. He inclined her head and led her a few paces down the hall. They were still close enough to see Danny's room, but far enough from the nurse's station to not be overheard.

"I hope you didn't feel like you had to rush your visit."

"No. They're going to have PT come and work with him. Get him on his feet a little." She shifted her weight. "What about the break-in at my house? Any luck there?"

"Unfortunately not. Whoever broke in did everything they could to cover their tracks. No fingerprints on the window they broke, and nothing else happened in the neighborhood that we could tie them to." He gave her an apologetic look. "I'm sorry, Leslie. Let's hope it was just a random burglary attempt that was interrupted when you got home."

Leslie knew she couldn't hide her disappointment. He was probably right, and it was a random one-time thing. Even if she knew one hundred percent that that was true, it was going to take a while before she would feel completely at ease going into her house at the end of her shifts.

"Someone should be at the house in a couple of hours to put in a new window. I'm having security lights installed at the front and back doors, too. You know, the kind that turn on when there's movement. I considered getting a quote on a security system, but I know it's out of my price range right now."

She wished she had a dog. A large dog with a booming bark. She'd always wanted one, but since she was on shift for a full twenty-four hours at a time, it would never work. Maybe one day, in the distant future, that could change.

"The security lights are a great idea. Something like that is often enough to discourage someone from messing with a house. We'll have extra patrols in your neighborhood for the next few days, too. I know it doesn't seem like much..."

"No, I appreciate it. Thank you."

Leslie's stomach growled. She'd grabbed a granola bar on the way out of the house this morning. She hadn't picked anything up when she took Becca to the cafeteria, but all of the food had smelled delicious. Maybe she should swing through a drive through and grab a burger on the way back to the house to meet the technician. She considered asking Clint if he wanted to join her for a quick lunch but stopped herself. He was on duty, and he surely had a list of things he had to do next.

The elevator just down from them dinged, and an older woman got out with a small bouquet of flowers in her arms. The vase was light purple, and it was filled with white roses and carnations along with some beautiful little lavender-colored flowers that matched the vase. Baby's breath filled out the rest of the bouquet.

The woman was dressed in the uniform of a hospital volunteer, including a name tag that had Gloria printed on it. She passed them and paused at the door to Danny's room where the posted officer stopped her.

The bright smile on the woman's face shifted to confusion. "I've got flowers for Leslie Granger, room 112."

Leslie exchanged a surprised glance with Clint. "I'm Leslie. Do you know who they're from?"

"I have no idea. I just deliver flowers." She smiled brightly again as she handed over the bouquet. "Maybe they signed the card? Have a great day." With that, she waved and disappeared back into the elevator.

Leslie held the bouquet away from her and breathed in the heavenly scent of the flowers. The carnations were especially strong.

"I take it you weren't expecting flowers?"

"Most certainly not, and especially not here. This makes no sense." She moved to a small table next to a couple of chairs and set the vase down. Clint followed her. A large envelope was held in place by a floral pick. The only thing written on the envelope was her name and the room number. Leslie retrieved the envelope and pulled the card out.

On the front were the typed words, "Never Forgotten."

When Leslie opened the card, there was nothing written inside. Instead, there was a photograph folded in half. She opened it up and gasped. It slipped from her hand and fluttered to land face up on the floor at her feet.

It was a picture of her reading nook.

From inside her house.

Chapter Ten

The moment Clint saw what was in the photo, his blood boiled. The intruder had violated Leslie's space, taken pictures, and was now using that to target her. And for what purpose? To show he had some level of control? Just to frighten her? Because they'd certainly accomplished that.

She'd barely said a handful of words since she first accepted the bouquet of flowers at the hospital. Now they were at the police station where he'd shown her to a quiet conference room. She filled out an official report and was now nursing a cup of coffee that Tia, one of their dispatch personnel and self-appointed barista in residence, had brought her.

Clint sat down in the chair beside hers. "I took the flowers and the note down to the lab for processing. I was hoping the flowers had come from the hospital gift shop. Instead, a man brought them into the hospital wearing a sweatshirt with the hood pulled up over his head. He told the volunteer it was supposed to be a surprise and wondered if she'd deliver the flowers for him. She didn't think anything of it and agreed to help."

Leslie set her coffee down on the table and pressed her first fingers against her temples. "And the hood prevented the cameras from getting a good look him."

"Yep. This isn't the guy's first rodeo. The volunteer couldn't see his face well, either, but she said he was white, middle aged, and five foot seven or five foot eight. She also commented that he wore black leather gloves."

"Which means the lab isn't likely to pull fingerprints off the flowers or the note."

He hated the defeated undertone in her voice. Even still, she wasn't wrong. At least they knew more about the person who broke into her home than they did this morning. He told her as much.

"The volunteer said the man already knew which room to have the flowers delivered to. Which means he got that information somehow. We're going to go through footage from the hospital and see if anyone wearing a hoodie like that came through before. Maybe asked about Danny."

Leslie slowly exhaled and leaned back in her chair. "Yeah. That's a good idea."

"We do need to talk about another possibility that we're considering—"

A knock at the conference room door interrupted him and drew their attention. Paris walked in and addressed Leslie.

"I'm Detective John Paris. I'm the officer assigned to Danny Bracken's case. I wanted to introduce myself and say that I was sorry to hear about the trouble you've been having." He circled the table and sat in a chair opposite Leslie. "You've had your personal space invaded. No one should have to deal with that."

"I appreciate that." She pulled her brown hair together at the base of her neck then pulled it around to flow over one shoulder. "Everything that's happened in the last twenty-four hours has been a nightmare."

Paris caught Clint's eye, and Clint shook his head. He hadn't had a chance to talk to her about their latest suspicion.

"Between the shooting, the break-in at your home, and now the flowers, it's hard to believe it's all just a coincidence." The detective leaned forward and rested his forearms on the table. "I think we need to consider the possibility that the man who shot Bracken may be the same one who's targeting you now."

Leslie's hand dropped to the arm of her chair, and she looked from Paris to Clint and back again. Her brow wrinkled. "That can't be possible. I was right there in the warehouse, and he aimed at Danny. If he was targeting me for some reason, why not just shoot me then? Or wait in the house and take me out when I got home? It doesn't make any sense."

Clint ignored the irrational instinct to reach over and cover her hand with his. To offer her some kind of emotional support. It would be completely unprofessional, not to mention she might not appreciate the gesture. He wished she had someone here to support her, like her sister or a close friend.

"You're right. It doesn't make any sense." The detective leaned away from the table. "The thing is, we're clearly missing a big part of this puzzle. Which means we'll have to try different pieces to see what fits and what doesn't until we get a clearer picture. We're waiting on several things right now. Any one of those will hopefully get us even closer to some concrete answers."

"What am I supposed to do in the meantime?" She glanced at the large clock on the wall. "I need to get back to my house. Technicians will be by in the next forty minutes to replace the broken window."

Clint had already spoken about the situation with both Paris and Chief Dolman. "If you have no objections, I'd like to accompany you. I can help keep an eye on things today. Hopefully having someone else around will deter the suspect from bothering you again."

For now. The truth was, Clint would prefer it if Leslie wasn't outside in the open any more than necessary. If they were right, and the shooter was the same man who was terrorizing Leslie, then he had a gun and knew how to use it. Clint didn't want her exposed.

Paris nodded. "We'll have someone posted outside your house tonight, too. We want to make sure you—and the Brackens—are safe."

Leslie certainly didn't have to agree to the arrangement, but Clint prayed that she would. The idea of her being at the house without someone there to watch her back bothered him more than he cared to admit.

She shifted in her chair and cleared her throat. "Yeah. That would be great. Thank you. Both of you."

"Good." Detective Paris stood. "And we appreciate your help and cooperation. We're going to figure this out, Miss Granger. I can promise you that." With that, he left the room again.

Clint's gaze swung to Leslie's face. She didn't look completely convinced, but the flash of hope he saw in her eyes was encouraging.

"Do you have someone coming to install the security lighting?"

"No. I'd planned to run into the home improvement

store on the south side—I always forget the name—and pick them up. I figured I'd install them myself if it wasn't too difficult, or I can always hire someone if necessary." She glanced at the clock again. "I'm not sure there'll be time to go by before the glass technicians arrive."

"Maybe not. But we can look online while they're replacing the glass, order what you need, and then swing by and pick it up. I'm more than happy to help you get everything installed."

He would've missed her moment of hesitation had he not been watching for her reaction. With a nod, she rolled her chair away from the conference table and stood. "I would actually really appreciate your help. Thank you again."

"You're welcome. Come on, let's get out of here and to your place before they arrive with the new window." He touched the middle of her back and guided her to the door.

He followed Leslie to her house and then asked her to wait while he quickly checked the house to make sure no one else was inside. Once it had been cleared, he escorted her in.

An hour later, the technicians were working on replacing the glass in the window, and he and Leslie were seated at the little wooden table in her dining room looking at security options on her laptop.

"I was thinking this light would be good for both the front and back doors." She clicked on the listing to bring up the description.

Clint had heard of the brand before and nodded. "That'll work well."

"Okay." She added two of them to her online shopping cart. "I was looking at these little window alarms, too. I know they're nothing fancy, but I'd sleep a whole lot better if I knew that, should someone break into my house again, I'd at least be warned." She raised her shoulders against a visible shiver. "What do you think?"

He preferred full security systems complete with video cameras, but that was not only a major investment, but it wasn't likely something they could get installed today. An alarm would hopefully scare an intruder away. Anything to discourage someone from breaking into Leslie's house or bothering her was a win in his book.

"Get one for each window. They should also sell stickers that let people know there's a security system in place. You can put one near each door. Simply seeing that might be enough to keep him—or anyone else—from messing with your place."

"That's a good idea." She added enough of the window alarms to cover all the windows in her home and then chose several stickers to put up on the outside of her house. "Can you think of anything else?"

He really couldn't. "I think you should be good to go."

She paid for the items and was told she'd receive an e-mail when they were ready to pick up. With that, she closed the laptop and rested her hands on the table. "Now what?"

"We wait."

For the window to get installed.

To pick up the security supplies.

For the suspect to strike again.

Chapter Eleven

W hen Clint said he could get the security lights installed for her, he wasn't kidding. It would've taken her so much longer to get one of them put up than it did for him to install both. Not only that, but he'd done it all without complaint or hesitation.

When he'd suggested following her back to the house and staying with her for the rest of the day, she wasn't sure she liked the idea. Truthfully, it was the thought of being at the house alone that had led to her agreement.

She'd had the opportunity to speak with him numerous times in the past, but it was always related to an emergency where they'd both been called to respond. They were an efficient team. Truth be told, when she saw him on a scene she was working, it usually brightened her day a little. A fact she'd never allowed herself to analyze too closely.

Now that they were in the same house—in the same room—and working together to install the window alarms, she had the opportunity to watch him work. He handled himself with confidence but included her in everything. He probably knew that helping would make her feel more in control of her situation.

In some respects, their training wasn't all that different. They'd both been taught how to deescalate a situation and keep the victim focused and calm.

Except she refused to think of herself as a victim because that meant the guy who was trying to shake her up was winning.

He wasn't going to win.

"All right, I'm ready for the last one."

Leslie opened the final package of mini alarms and dropped the pieces into the palm of his hand. By now, they knew exactly how to put them on the windows, and it took less than a minute before the last window was armed.

She observed their work, her hands perched on her hips, and nodded with satisfaction. It wouldn't keep anyone from breaking into her house again, but it would keep it from being a surprise. They'd tested each alarm to make sure they worked, and there was no missing the warning sound. It'd wake her up from a dead sleep without question.

Between that and barricading the doors when she was home for the night, she hoped and prayed he wouldn't be getting back into her house again.

"Thank you. I feel a lot better about staying here tonight." She gathered up the trash and stuffed it back into the plastic bag the alarms had come in. When she looked up, she caught Clint watching her.

He tried to conceal the look of concern on his face, but he wasn't quick enough. He must've realized it because he explained himself.

"I really wish you could stay with someone else until we get these cases wrapped up. Are you sure you can't call your sister? Or do you have another friend or family member who could stay here with you?"

"Please trust me when I say that staying at my sister's isn't an option. We don't get along well enough to live in the same house. Not to mention, if I've got someone coming after me, I don't want to paint a target on my sister or my nieces." She'd never forgive herself if something happened to them. "As for friends? Again, I can't ask them to come here and put themselves at risk. Now if someone had a big dog I could borrow for a few days..." She chuckled. "I'm picturing a giant Great Dane lounging on my couch. I think I'd have to get another one, or there wouldn't be enough room for me."

Clint laughed. "I can't picture you with a Great Dane."

"Please don't tell me you think I'm a little dog kind of person."

"No." He ran a hand over his bearded chin. "I was thinking more like a Doberman or a rottweiler. One of those tough breeds that can handle anything, people know not to mess with them, but when it comes to friends or family, they're sweet and loyal. It would be a good fit for you, since you're tough, too."

"Wow, you put a lot of thought into that." His compliment made her cheeks warm. She ducked her chin. "I appreciate that. I'm not sure how strong I am, though."

"Everyone hits rough patches when they aren't sure whether they can handle what's ahead. But you? You got back up, kept going, and still worried about others in the process. If that's not tough, I don't know what is."

His gaze held hers for several moments until his phone rang, the sound echoing through the living room and effectively interrupting their conversation.

Leslie crossed her arms in front of her and moved to perch on the edge of the couch as he answered.

"This is Baker." He listened to whoever was on the other end of the line for several moments before speaking again. "I appreciate that, Chief Menendez. I'll be by shortly. Bye."

She figured he was talking to someone else at the police station. She hadn't expected it to be her own chief. "Is everything okay with Danny?"

"What? Oh, Chief Menendez was looking into several things for me. Mostly with regards to possible missing equipment that the shooter may have stolen. He said he could get everything e-mailed over, but I'd like to talk to him in person. Get his take on whatever he found out."

Leslie jumped to her feet. "I'd like to go with you." Anything was better than sitting around the house by herself waiting for something to happen.

"I was going to suggest the same. Let's put those security alarm stickers on the doors and head out. We can grab something for dinner afterward. Should we take something back to the hospital for Danny and Becca?"

That Clint had thought about them warmed her heart. "No, we've got a schedule set up. Someone else will take dinner to them tonight. I've been assigned tomorrow night."

"It's a good thing when people are there for each other like that. It's similar at the precinct. Everyone looks out for each other. Tia's usually in charge of the meal train and the prayer chain. We never turn down a reason to celebrate."

"Neither do we. We're like a family." Something that Leslie, with very little family of her own, certainly appreciated. Sometimes she felt closer to the people she worked with than she did her own sister.

That feeling stuck with her as they pulled up to the fire

station. Sure, she always looked forward to her days off when she could relax, get some good sleep, and catch up on things. But she never dreaded going back to work. She loved being a firefighter and helping others when they were experiencing some of their worst moments.

She got out of Clint's patrol car and led the way into the station. It took a few minutes to make their way to the chief's office as she was stopped and greeted by multiple co-workers. Some of them she didn't always see because they were on different shifts.

"We're praying for Danny."

"Let us know if you need anything."

Leslie smiled and thanked everyone for their kindness.

They didn't need to knock on Chief Menendez's door. Instead, he waved them in and motioned for them to close the door. They exchanged pleasantries as she and Clint took seats.

The chief didn't waste any time once they were settled. He picked up a blue folder and handed it to Clint. "I went through and compiled a list of every call we've been on in the last year where someone was hurt or killed. I also included those that led to an investigation by the PD. I imagine you'll have more details on those cases."

"This is great. Thank you." Clint opened the folder.

Leslie counted at least a dozen papers tucked in there. She tried to think through the different calls they'd had over the last year. Thankfully, the instances where they couldn't help someone in time, or where someone was already injured or worse when they got there, were few. Still, it was smart to take a second look at them. She hoped Clint would let her look through them. Maybe something would jog a memory that could be helpful.

Clint nodded. "This is very thorough. I appreciate the assistance. Did you find anything about the equipment?"

Chief Menendez's expression tightened. "I reached out to each of the stations in town and had them go through their equipment and list anything that was missing. There's nearly an entire set of personal protective equipment missing from station four, including a self-contained breathing apparatus."

Leslie gasped. "How did that happen?" Each firefighter was required to keep track of, clean, and store away their own gear. If any of them misplaced their equipment... well, she wasn't sure how bad it would be because, as long as she'd been working for the department, it hadn't happened.

"That's not all." Chief Menendez folded his hands together and rested them on the top of his desk. "We may have discovered a potential suspect: a firefighter who was deemed unfit for duty at the same station."

Chapter Twelve

W hen Chief Menendez mentioned they might have a possible suspect, Leslie stared at her boss in disbelief. "Another firefighter? How's that possible? Even if he was considered unfit for duty, how could targeting other firefighters possibly accomplish anything?"

Clint completely understood her reluctance to believe something like that could happen. But he'd seen it himself in the police department two years ago when one of their officers had been working with a local drug cartel. They hadn't seen it coming, and it'd nearly led to the death of another officer. The betrayal had been real and extremely difficult for the whole precinct to grasp.

Chief Menendez looked equally displeased about the possibility. He pulled another file out and slid it across the desk. "Domingo Ortiz. There'd been some question about his mental fitness after his psychological evaluation, but nothing that could be pinpointed. He passed that and then made it through the fire academy by the skin of his teeth.

However, he was caught stealing from the station. Mostly food that he swore were leftovers and that he was giving to a family member who didn't have enough to eat."

While certainly not ideal—there had to be a better way of making sure his family ate—that didn't seem like enough grounds to let Ortiz go. "I take it he started to diversify his acquisitions."

"You could say that. Office supplies began to go missing, then small electronics. A fellow firefighter's smart watch, a video game cartridge for the station's gaming system, things like that. He was finally caught when, during his shift, he was handing off a set of turnout gear to a friend in the parking lot." Menendez lifted an eyebrow. "Needless to say, that was the end of that. He was re-evaluated by a psychologist and found to have issues with impulse control and was officially diagnosed with kleptomania."

Leslie leaned toward Clint and scanned the open file on the desk in front of them. "I don't remember ever meeting this man before. All of this was almost a year ago. Do we have any idea how long the set of gear had been missing?"

"It's been at least a month. Beyond that, though, we don't know." Chief Menendez frowned, the lines at the corners of his mouth deepening. "The fact we didn't even know the gear was missing is something that'll be addressed in a separate internal investigation."

There were so many factors at play here. It sounded extremely likely that Ortiz was the one who took the gear. Did he take it to keep for himself, or did he try to sell it to make some money? Admittedly, Clint knew very little about kleptomania and made a mental note to speak to their station's resident psychologist for more insight.

"We're going to need to contact Ortiz and question

him." Clint tapped the file. "Is the address you show here still current?"

"It's the last known address we had for him. But it's certainly possible he's moved on since then. I doubt very much he would have sent us a change of address card."

"I'd like to speak to people who worked with him at station four. Is there a best way to go about that?"

Menendez tapped his cell phone. "I'll give them a call and let them know to expect you." He shifted his gaze to Leslie. "Chief Caradec is going to be feeling defensive enough about the gear being stolen without his knowledge. It might be helpful if another firefighter were there, too."

"Understood, sir."

"How are *you* doing, Granger? I heard about your house."

Clint and Leslie had spoken about how much they should share with the chief. Right now, they knew so little that Clint wasn't too worried about it. Besides, if she told her boss what was going on, it'd give more grounds for extra time off if that's what was needed to keep her safe until they found the man responsible for everything.

She updated Menendez on the break-in and the flowers and picture. Then she quickly turned the topic to Bracken and her visit with him. "He seemed to be in good spirits, sir, although I can tell he's in pain. Hopefully that will diminish a lot over the next few days."

"I hope so, too." He focused on Clint. "I trust you'll continue to keep me updated on the investigation."

"I will. You may also hear from Detective John Paris. We don't have enough details yet, and we don't even know if Ortiz is involved in this. However, there's enough evidence to suggest firefighters in general may be the target, if not Bracken and Granger specifically. I hope all your people are exercising caution moving forward."

"We are, and I appreciate your concern. If there's anything I can do to aid the investigation, please let me know."

They said goodbye to the fire chief and were on their way out of the station when someone called Leslie from across the room.

"Hey, Granger! Catch!"

The man launched something at her, and she easily snatched it out of the air. When she opened her hand, a package of plain M&Ms rested in her palm.

"Figured you could use it after yesterday. Be safe out there."

"You know it. Thanks, Allen."

The other firefighter saluted and returned to work.

"So you really are a chocolate addict, and everyone knows it." Clint chuckled as he opened the door for her then went around and got behind the wheel.

"Yep." She tore the package open. "There are worse things I could be addicted to. Besides, there are health benefits to chocolate. Probably when consumed in smaller amounts than I eat, but still." She laughed softly as she tilted the bag in his direction.

"Very true." He shook a handful into his palm and tossed them into his mouth. "I don't know about an addiction, but I can never go into a gas station and pass up those fried beef and bean burritos."

Leslie's nose wrinkled automatically, causing Clint to dish out an offended look.

She quickly swallowed the M&Ms she was chewing and held up a hand in repentance. "I'm sorry. I wasn't trying to judge. It just seems like they're always at least a day or two old."

"Hey, they're delicious. And like I said, I only get them when I stop at a gas station. I don't have fellow officers throwing burritos at me when I go into the precinct."

She tilted her head back and laughed, her hazel eyes sparkling. "Touché."

She looked happy. Carefree. Beautiful.

Right then, Clint wanted nothing more than to find the man responsible for shooting Bracken and breaking into Leslie's house. He wanted her to feel safe again.

A section of hair fell down the right side of her face, and he had to make a point of not reaching over to brush it aside.

As if she somehow knew what he was thinking, she hooked a finger and swept the hair behind her ear before popping several blue M&Mss into her mouth. "So, what's next?"

"I think we should head over and talk to Chief Caradec. Maybe talk to a few of the firefighters who worked with Ortiz and see what they thought about the guy. Before we do that, though, I'm going to update Detective Paris. I'm hoping he'll reach out to a psychologist we work with, Dr. Gerard, and see what information he can give us about kleptomania and what we might expect if Ortiz is our suspect."

"That sounds like a good plan." She settled back into her seat and ate a few more M&Ms while he made that call.

Paris said he'd contact Dr. Gerard and get back to them once they'd been able to speak. When Clint ended the call, Leslie tucked the package into one of the side pockets in the small backpack she'd brought along with her. "What happens if we don't figure out who's behind this?"

"Then we keep looking for clues. Waiting for him to

mess up." He glanced over at her to find her nibbling on her lower lip. "We're going to find him, Leslie."

"What if it takes a while? What happens when Danny is discharged from the hospital? Will an officer continue to keep an eye on his house and family?"

"We're not going to let anything happen to them." Her unspoken question seemed to echo in the space between them. "And I'm not going to let anything happen to you, either."

Chapter Thirteen

Menendez had been right. Chief Caradec wasn't especially thrilled to welcome Clint into his office, but when Leslie introduced herself, a little of that stony exterior seemed to crack. She couldn't blame him, though. If someone entered her station with potential accusations, she'd be on the defensive as well. The men and women she worked with were a family of sorts, and they protected their own.

"I wish I could tell you exactly when the equipment went missing. It's been at least a month. But Ortiz was dismissed a year ago, so if he is the one who took it, I don't understand why the delay." Chief Caradec stood from his chair and crossed the room to a window that overlooked the area in front of station six. "We had several sets of gear that we retired either due to wear and tear, or because it had been more than ten years since it was manufactured. Very little of it was still serviceable and was sent to be disposed of." He turned and leaned against the windowsill. "Clearly someone did take the gear, but it had to be somewhere between here and its destination. If it was Ortiz, he didn't

83

leave on a good note. There's no way he could've gotten back into the station without someone noticing and reporting the incident."

It'd be nearly impossible to determine at what point the equipment had been swiped. Even if it had been caught on camera, that was an almost impossible amount of footage to go through.

Leslie nodded her head, hoping that Caradec would understand that they were on his side. "What were your impressions of Ortiz?"

Caradec shook his head as if he still couldn't believe it all happened in the first place. "He was a nice enough guy. He made it through everything—the medical examinations, the interviews, the evaluations, and the academy—but all by a narrow margin. He wasn't especially personable, but then not everyone can be the class clown. People either seemed to really like him, or they were offended by him. There wasn't much in between. To be honest, I had my doubts when he started working here but wanted to give him a chance. Everyone deserves that much."

Clint made several notes. "How long did he serve here?"

"It wasn't quite eight months. We started noticing things would go missing maybe two months after he came on board. They were little things that we kept chalking up to accidents or a prank. Things that didn't really matter in the long run like the stapler or pepper shaker. That went on for several months. I think we all suspected something was going on, but we couldn't prove it. It wasn't until a smart watch and a framed photo disappeared that I knew there was more to it." Caradec returned to his chair and sat down. "We tried to catch the thief in action. I'll hand it to Ortiz. The guy was good. We didn't catch him until he was trying to carry a set of turnout gear to a buddy parked behind the station."

Clint tapped the back of his pen against his notepad. "Did he ever admit to the thefts?"

"Yes. I have to give him credit for that. It wouldn't be easy to stand in front of your peers and admit that you stole from them. Not only that, but he swore that he felt so guilty each time that he'd either given everything away or tossed it. Said he didn't deserve to keep them for himself."

Leslie frowned. For some of those personal items that had been stolen, it must have been frustrating and disheartening to know they might have simply been tossed into the garbage.

Caradec cleared his throat and continued. "Needless to say, he lost his job that day. Ortiz seemed devastated, and we quickly learned about his kleptomania. He ended up checking into a rehab facility for a while. Honestly, it didn't seem right to press charges at the time. Now, however, I'm thinking we probably should have. Either way, he'll never work as a firefighter again. I haven't seen or spoken to him in almost a year."

That seemed to satisfy Clint. He made several more notes then slipped his notepad into a pocket along with his pen. "Is there anyone on duty now who worked with him? If so, we'd like to speak to them. Get their impressions as well. If you don't think it'd be too much of a disturbance."

They ended up talking to three different firefighters who had worked directly with Ortiz. All had similar reports to what Caradec said. Ortiz was an odd guy who either really connected with another person or came off as annoying or obnoxious. None of them suspected kleptomania until it'd officially come to light. If there was one thing everyone agreed on, it was that they couldn't picture the man becoming violent.

Leslie had thought this visit to station six would bring some things into perspective. Instead, she came away feeling even more confused.

"It's quite a jump to go from kleptomania to arson and attempted murder." Apparently, Clint had been thinking along the same lines. "I'm sure it's possible. A lot can happen in a year—a year in Ortiz's life that we know nothing about."

She looked at the time. It was after five in the evening. "What now? We wait?"

"Unfortunately, it's all we can do."

It was not knowing how long they were going to have to wait for answers that got to Leslie. "I need to check in with my sister and see how she's doing. She's had a rough go of it lately, and my brother-in-law is likely out of town again."

"Wow, it must be hard on her with him gone so much."

"It is. His workaholic tendencies are a sore subject between them. I do my best to try and stay out of it, but it's not always easy."

Clint looked like he wanted to say something else and thought better of it. "How do you and your sister feel about fried chicken?"

His question was so random that Leslie stared at him for a moment.

He laughed, the sound rumbly and low. "We could go by and pick up a bucket and sides and take it by your sister's place. Eat there, if you want to."

"That's actually a very sweet idea. The thing is, Cindy doesn't know a whole lot about what's going on. I told her about Danny, and I'm sure she's seen some of that on the news. I also texted her today and told her about the break-in at my house." She pulled the seatbelt over her shoulder and secured it. "I haven't mentioned anything about the creepy picture or that there might be a connection between what's going on with me and what happened at the warehouse."

"I won't say a word. But if you feel like my being there might make her worry, I completely understand."

Her nieces would probably get a kick out of eating dinner with a real police officer, especially since Clint was wearing his uniform. It'd be good to see Cindy and the girls. Plus, she was starving.

"Let me call and make sure she doesn't have any other plans."

Cindy had been about to make macaroni and cheese for dinner and apparently the opportunity to have a conversation with other adults sounded like heaven. She jumped at the idea. Leslie had been right—Peter was out of town for the next three days.

Half an hour later, they arrived at Cindy's house. They'd barely pulled up to the curb when the front door slammed open and five-year-old Izzy came running down the walkway, her bare feet slapping the concrete.

Leslie got out of the car and scooped her niece into her arms. "You must've been watching for us, huh?"

Izzy nodded but kept her wide eyes on Clint as he got out of the car and started pulling bags of food from the back seat. "Who's that?"

"That's my friend, Officer Clint."

"Izzy! What have I told you about closing the door behind you?" Cindy stood in the open doorway, her hands on her hips, and two-year-old Bree in her arms. "Your sister could follow you and get hurt or lost."

"Sorry, Mama." Izzy spared her mom a glance as Leslie set her back down.

Clint closed the door and smiled down at the little girl. "Do you want to help me bring the food in?"

Izzy looked up at him with wide eyes and nodded.

He handed her a small plastic bag with handles. She clutched it close and carefully carried it inside as though it might hold something precious.

Clint waited for Leslie to lead the way. As they approached the door, she introduced her sister and youngest niece.

"He's Auntie's boyfriend," Izzy declared as she marched right past her mom and into the house.

Chapter Fourteen

C lint did his best to keep a straight face as he carried the bags of food in behind the adorable little girl. Her declaration clearly embarrassed her aunt because poor Leslie's face was bright red. He didn't want her to feel self-conscious, but goodness she was gorgeous when she blushed.

He remembered rolling his eyes and groaning when his dad said a man should always find new ways to make his bride blush. Dad certainly took that to heart, and Mom never seemed to mind.

Clint never understood that—until now. He wouldn't mind seeing Leslie blush on a regular basis.

Intentionally shoving such ridiculous thoughts from his head, he set the bags down on the oval-shaped table in the dining room and turned to greet Cindy properly with a handshake. "Hey, it's nice to meet you."

"You, too." Even Cindy's cheeks were pink. "Don't worry, I'll have a talk with her later." She glared at her oldest daughter who had no clue she'd done anything wrong.

Instead, she climbed into one of the chairs and bounced up and down on her knees in anticipation. "Mama said you were bringing fried chicken. I *love* fried chicken."

Cindy set Bree down. The little girl took one look at Clint and ran to Leslie, who happily picked her up.

"I do too, pumpkin." Cindy affectionately tugged on her daughter's little ponytail. "Why don't you help me by getting some napkins and putting five of them on the table."

"Okay." Izzy hopped back down again and bounced over to the counter.

Clint chuckled. "She's got a lot of energy."

"Oh, you have *no* idea." Leslie lifted the younger girl in her arms. "So does this one, but she's a little shy when she first meets new people. She's also on the tail end of an ear infection, so that slows her down a little." She patted her niece's back. "Come on, honey, let's get you set up in your highchair."

It was momentarily chaotic, but soon they were all sitting around the table. Clint found himself between Leslie and Izzy.

Cindy started to pray over their food and immediately, Izzy rested her little hand in his palm. A glance around the table told him that it was customary for the family to hold hands during prayer. He reached for Leslie's and held it loosely in his.

When the prayer ended, she withdrew her hand, and they focused on fixing their plates. Everyone enjoyed the meal, and even little Bree asked for a second spoonful of mashed potatoes and gravy.

"That's my favorite part, too," he told her with a wink.

It'd taken most of the meal, but she finally stopped avoiding his gaze and gave him a big grin. White gravy rimmed her lips.

She was a cute little thing and looked just like her mom. Izzy, on the other hand, looked nothing like them. He had to assume she must take after her father. A man who, from what Leslie had mentioned and the little comments the girls made, must not make it home for dinner very often.

Leslie and Cindy managed dinner and getting the girls cleaned up like a well-oiled machine. While they did that, Clint cleared the table, took the trash out, and washed the few dishes they'd used.

He was just placing the last plate in the dish drainer when Cindy walked in. She hitched an eyebrow. "A man in uniform and he knows how to do the dishes. It's a wonder you're still single, especially here in Destiny."

"Cindy! Really?" Leslie entered the kitchen then and gave her sister a withering look.

Cindy only shrugged and left the room, saying she needed to check on the girls.

Leslie's gaze shifted to him. The adorable blush was back. "You'll have to excuse my sister. Sometimes she doesn't know when to hold her tongue."

"I don't mind. She's nice. So are your nieces. I'm glad I had the chance to meet them." He folded a towel lengthwise and draped it over the top of the cabinet door below the sink. "It looks like you guys are pretty close."

"We are more now than we used to be." Leslie lowered her voice. "We haven't always gotten along. Sometimes we still don't. But once the girls were born and Peter was gone all the time... Well, I guess we figured out how to work around that. Necessity and all." She pointed to the clock on the microwave. "It's after seven. We should go so Cindy can get the girls ready for bed."

"Yeah. Of course."

They found the trio in the living room where Izzy was

busy building with oversized Lego bricks and Cindy was rocking Bree.

"I think we're going to head out," Leslie announced. "Thanks for letting us stop by."

Cindy reached one arm up and gave her a hug as Leslie leaned down. "Thank you for bringing dinner. It was delicious."

Izzy skipped over and gave Clint a hug. "You *are* my auntie's boyfriend, right?"

Cindy and Leslie both audibly sighed. Leslie knelt to her niece's level.

"Honey, Officer Clint is my friend. And now he's your friend, too."

Izzy's eyes narrowed as though she were trying to figure something out. "And he's a boy. So he's your boyfriend."

"Hard to argue with that logic," Clint muttered under his breath. It was all he could do not to laugh.

The sun had gone down by the time they left Cindy's house. They'd barely gotten to the car when Detective Paris sent a message saying Dr. Gerard was on his way to the station to consult with them about Ortiz and kleptomania. They were buckled up and headed straight over.

Clint glanced over at Leslie in the passenger seat. He could see her profile against the light coming in from outside.

"Izzy is a hoot."

"She's something, all right." Humor laced Leslie's voice. "She gives Cindy a run for her money. What about your brother? Does he have a family?"

"Drew. Yeah, he and Emma have been married for five

years now. No kids, though. There have been several miscarriages. I think they're considering adoption, although I don't think they've begun the process yet."

"I'm sorry to hear about their losses. I can only imagine how heartbreaking that must be."

"Thank you." The last miscarriage earlier in the year had happened in the second trimester. It'd been devastating. Clint hated seeing his brother and sister-in-law hurting so deeply.

Even through it all, their relationship had remained strong. It reminded Clint of the ones their parents had. That kind of connection was what Clint desperately wanted to experience himself. To find someone he could share his life with no matter what the world threw their way.

The problem was, even though he'd been on his fair share of dates over the years, he'd never met the one woman that both challenged and intrigued him. Someone he could imagine growing old with.

Until now.

He wasn't naïve. He didn't know Leslie well enough to be in love with her. But he'd seen enough about her character and the way she tackled challenges in life to want to get to know her better.

The parking lot in front of the precinct was nearly empty as they parked and walked in. While Clint didn't particularly enjoy working late, it was usually easier to get work done when the bullpen wasn't as busy.

Clint escorted Leslie through part of the building and intercepted Detective Paris just outside the breakroom.

"You have perfect timing. Dr. Gerard just got here." He gave Leslie a welcoming smile. "I'm sorry, but you'll have to wait outside. This shouldn't take long."

"I understand. No worries."

Paris gave a satisfied nod and pointed to Clint. "Meet us in conference room three."

"Will do." He showed Leslie to the break room where there was a small table for her to sit at while she waited. He immediately went to one of the vending machines, put two dollars in, and hit the buttons for M&Ms. When the candy dropped down, he retrieved it and set it on the table in front of her. "Do you want something to drink? I can grab you a soda, too."

She looked up at him, her smile bright. "I'm good. Thank you for the candy. I'll just munch on that and read a book I've got on my phone. I'll be fine."

"Okay." He rested his hand on her shoulder, his thumb just grazing her neck. "I'll be back as soon as I can."

In the conference room, he claimed one of the chairs across from where Dr. Gerard and Paris were seated.

The first time he'd met the psychologist, he'd expected an older gentleman with wild hair and eyebrows. Something akin to Dr. Brown from the movie Back to the Future. Instead, Gerard was a man in his early forties whose thick, close-cut hair didn't show a hint of gray. Clint never would've guessed his profession if he'd run into him somewhere else.

Dr. Gerard folded his hands and rested them on the table. "I looked through everything you have on Domingo Ortiz, which wasn't a lot. As you know, it would take a warrant to gain access to the files concerning his stay at the rehabilitation facility."

"And since we have no solid proof that Ortiz stole the equipment or is involved in any of this, a warrant isn't in the immediate future." Paris nodded to Gerard. "I understand you may not be able to give us any insight into Ortiz specifically. But what can you tell us about individuals who struggle with kleptomania in general?"

Gerard took a drink from a water bottle near his elbow. "Kleptomania is a serious mental health disorder. Typically, individuals that suffer from this disorder have a powerful urge to steal items that they don't really need. The more they resist the urge to steal, the more tension and anxiety they may feel leading up to the theft. While stealing, or immediately afterward, they experience relief or satisfaction—an adrenaline rush similar to being high. Once that rush fades, they feel terrible guilt, self-loathing, shame, and fear of arrest."

That seemed to track with a lot of what Chief Caradec told them. "Ortiz's boss at the station where he worked said that Ortiz either gave away or trashed most of the items he'd stolen. Is that typical behavior?"

"Absolutely." Dr. Gerard leaned back in his chair. "When an individual with kleptomania steals something, it's not because they need or want that item. It's the act of stealing and the temporary relief it provides that drives them. Most of the time, they stash the stolen items away, gift them to family or friends, throw them in the trash, or even secretly return them because the guilt they feel is overwhelming."

Clint thought back over their conversation with Caradec. "I guess they finally figured out what Ortiz was doing when he tried to steal a set of turnout gear. He was attempting to pass it off to someone waiting for him outside when he was caught."

"Now that's interesting." Gerard leaned forward, his brows drawn together in thought. "With someone who has kleptomania, stealing is often spontaneous and almost never done with the help of someone else. That specific behavior doesn't track with everything else I'm hearing about Ortiz."

Paris looked encouraged by that bit of news. "Is it possible he was coerced into stealing the turnout gear? Maybe someone knew he was stealing and took advantage of the situation?"

"That's certainly possible. It also could be that he faked having kleptomania to cover what he'd really wanted to steal." Gerard shrugged. "It's impossible to know with the information we've been given. However, I'd be lying if I said it sounded like a cut and dried case of kleptomania."

They needed to hear what Ortiz had to say about the attempted theft of the gear. If the man either faked his diagnosis or was working with someone else, then that changed everything.

"I'll have him brought in for questioning tomorrow." Paris pointed at Clint. "I'll let you know when so you can be here."

"I appreciate that."

Paris reached over and shook Gerard's hand. "Thank you for taking the time to come speak with us. The information was invaluable."

"I'm happy to. I can come back when you question Ortiz if you'd like. If there's anything else I can do, please let me know."

Paris's cell phone rang. He waved goodbye to Dr. Gerard as he swiped to answer the call. "This is Detective Paris. That's great. We'll be there. Have a good night."

"Good news?" They could certainly use some.

"That was fire Chief Menendez. Would you please ask Miss Granger to join us?"

"Absolutely." Clint took out the folder Menendez had given him. He handed it to Paris. "Speaking of the chief, he gave this to me earlier. He'd compiled a list of call outs that involved a death or ended with the identification of an arsonist. Anything that might have given someone a reason to dislike the fire department."

Paris accepted the folder with a nod. "I appreciate it. I'll start going through this first thing tomorrow."

Clint found Leslie sitting at the table in the breakroom, an empty M&M package at her elbow.

She looked up from her phone. "That didn't take long."

"Dr. Gerard just left. Detective Paris got a call and wanted to speak with both of us."

"Of course." She tossed the candy wrapper into the trash and followed him back to the conference room.

"Ah, Miss Granger. Thank you for joining us." Paris sat on the edge of the conference table. "I received a call from Chief Menendez. It seems we've been cleared to go back into the warehouse and conduct a thorough search of the undamaged part of the building. It's my hope that we'll find some evidence that will tell us what happened to the shooter. If you feel up to it, I'd like you to be there, too. Your insight into where the shooting happened and what direction the suspect went would be a huge help."

Clint resisted the urge to reach over and place a hand against Leslie's back and offer his support. It wouldn't be easy for her to go back into the warehouse. But if she was nervous, she didn't let on. Instead, she straightened her spine and gave a definitive nod.

"I'll be happy to help in any way I can."

"Excellent. In that case, I'll see you both at the warehouse at 9 a.m."

Chapter Fifteen

It took some time for Leslie to register that the beeping in her dream was the sound of her alarm clock. She'd set it for seven a.m. after Clint had brought her back home last night. She wanted plenty of time to wake up, eat breakfast, and get ready to go through the warehouse.

After getting very little sleep, all she wanted to do was take the alarm clock and throw it into the wall. Instead, she turned it off with more force than necessary and groaned.

It'd taken a long time to finally relax enough to try and go to sleep the night before. She'd made popcorn, watched several episodes of one of her favorite shows, and even read for a while. It was after one in the morning when her head hit the pillow and, surprisingly, she'd fallen asleep immediately.

Unfortunately, that was also when the nightmares began. She relived that call to the warehouse. This time, though, she somehow knew what was going to happen next, and yet she and Danny followed that other firefighter into another room.

Powerless to stop it, she had to watch as Danny was shot

right in front of her, his body collapsing to the ground in slow motion.

Just like before, she managed to get him onto her shoulders. This time, though, she couldn't find her way out. She wandered through the dark warehouse as the smoke grew thicker and thicker, completely lost and unable to contact anyone else. She'd known time was running out for Danny, and there hadn't been anything she could do about it.

That's when Leslie finally woke up the first time, drenched in sweat and her cheeks wet with tears. It'd taken a change of pajamas, time spent reading her Bible and praying, and a cup of hot chocolate before she was able to go to sleep again after four in the morning.

If she did dream after that, she was thankful she didn't remember any of it.

She forced herself to get out of bed and flicked the bedroom light on. Although the sun would be peeking out over the horizon momentarily, it was still dark outside.

With a yawn, she made her way to the kitchen where she'd left the light on. It made her feel better knowing that someone couldn't sneak around the house in the dark at night.

She got dressed then cleaned up for the day. By the time she left her bedroom and headed for the kitchen, sunlight had started to stream through the cracks in the blinds.

She poured herself a glass of chocolate milk then fished around in the pantry until she found the blueberry protein bars she kept on hand when she didn't feel like making something for breakfast.

Her hands full, she went to the living room. She'd barely gotten comfortable on the couch when a text came through on her phone. She smiled when she saw Cindy's name and remembered dinner last night.

Are you up?

Yep.

Her phone rang a moment later. Leslie put it on speaker so she didn't have to hold onto the phone. "Good morning. How's Bree feeling today?"

"She didn't complain about her ear at bedtime. Hopefully that means the infection has cleared up. She's still asleep. So is Izzy. I think having company over last night wore them out."

Leslie imagined her sister was enjoying some time to herself this morning. "Well, it was fun to eat with you all. I think Clint got a big kick out of the girls—especially Izzy."

"Oh my word." Cindy groaned. "That child has no filter between what pops up inside her head and what pours out of her mouth."

"You're not going to hear me argue that point. It's endearing, though." She reached for her protein bar but set it back down with a wrinkle of her nose. She really wasn't in the mood to eat.

"Maybe right now it is, but it won't be in another year or two. I've been trying to explain when it's appropriate to speak up, and when it's better to just hold your tongue. It's not an easy thing to convey, though, when the differences aren't always black and white." It sounded like Cindy took a drink of something and set the glass back on the table. "Thanks again for bringing dinner by."

"No problem. It was nice to have a break from everything going on." Silence followed for several moments, and Leslie was starting to wonder whether the line had been cut off. "Are you still there?"

"Clint seems really nice."

Uh, oh. Leslie knew that big sister tone well.

"Yeah, he is. He and the entire Destiny police department have been awesome ever since Danny was hurt." That was totally *not* what Cindy was trying to get at.

"You guys have a connection. I can tell he'd be good for you, Les. Maybe it's time you started to date again. See someone seriously for a change."

Leslie bit back her response. She knew that Cindy had her best interests at heart. Dating had never come easily, and once she'd decided to become a firefighter, it had gotten even harder.

Women always seemed to swoon over a man in uniform. Especially when that man fought fires and rescued kittens from trees. But women firefighters? Yeah, they didn't quite have the same effect on men.

"I don't have a lot of time to date."

"You don't *take* the time to date," Cindy corrected. She wasn't wrong. "He's interested in you. Just promise me you'll think about it, okay? You guys both get the crazy hours and the inherent danger that comes with what you do. There's a lot to be said for that."

"Yeah. There is." She suppressed a sigh. "I don't know. Maybe once this case is over and things go back to normal... I promise I'll think about it."

They talked for another ten minutes before Izzy woke up and Cindy needed to go.

Even though Leslie tried to focus on the book she was reading, she couldn't get what her sister said out of her head.

Was Cindy right when she said Clint was interested in her? The possibility caused her pulse to pick up speed because, if she were honest with herself, she was attracted to him, too.

Doubt clouded in, though, when she reminded herself of their current situation. She didn't want to confuse his possible innate need to protect her with an interest that was anything more than that of a kind police officer who was looking out for her.

Leslie sighed, and she tried to focus on the morning ahead. No matter what she did, flashes of last night's dream kept coming to mind. She wasn't one to have anxiety attacks, but what if she got to the warehouse and couldn't make herself go back in again?

She unleashed a groan of frustration. "Please, Lord, calm my mind. Help me focus on something I *can* control."

Her phone rang, and when she saw Clint's name on the screen, the anticipation of talking to him displaced her nerves just a little. "Good morning."

"Good morning. I, uh... I don't want to overstep here, but I was wondering if you'd eaten breakfast yet."

Her gaze fell on the unopen protein bar, and she almost laughed. "No, I haven't."

"How would you feel if I brought some donuts over? We could eat, then maybe drive over to the warehouse together."

Having Clint here would make it a lot easier to forget about the dream. Maybe she could focus on something else besides the memories that kept swirling inside her head. She sent up a silent prayer of thanks for the distraction. "Are you kidding? That sounds great."

"Oh, good." He sounded relieved. "Because I already bought them, and I'm parked out front."

Leslie laughed as she unlocked the door and pulled it open. He ended the call, and she slipped her phone into her pocket.

He approached the door with a large box of donuts in

his hands and a sheepish grin on his face. Once inside, he set the box on the table. "Hey."

"Hey. So, what would you have done with all these donuts if I'd already eaten breakfast?"

Clint shrugged. "I guess the guys at the precinct would've been happy. Of course, you would've missed out on some chocolate donuts that look pretty amazing if I do say so myself." He lifted the lid to reveal a dozen pastries, and at least half of them were either chocolate, had chocolate frosting on top, or both.

Her stomach growled loudly in response.

"You know me well, sir."

"I try to pay attention to the things that matter."

Was he referring to her love of chocolate... or to her in general?

Her heart sped up in response to the possibility. He was watching her, a soft look in his eyes that had her frozen in place. Was it possible that Cindy was right, and that the attraction Leslie felt went both ways?

"I have chocolate milk," she blurted out, breaking the silence. "Oh, and orange juice. Do you have a preference?"

That wasn't awkward at all.

He chuckled. "Orange juice sounds great."

She nodded. She filled two glasses of orange juice and retrieved a couple of plates. They chose their donuts and moved the box to a kitchen counter so they'd have enough space to eat at the table.

Leslie took a bite of her chocolate donut with chocolate frosting and was immediately glad she'd abandoned her protein bar. *So. Good.*

Clint had chosen a cake donut with chocolate frosting. "Did you sleep okay last night?"

Since her mouth was still full, she simply shook her

head. Once she swallowed her bite, she washed it down with some juice. "Not particularly. I had nightmares."

"About the warehouse?"

She nodded, relieved when he didn't ask for details. Living through the dream last night was bad enough, she didn't really want to talk about it.

A change of topic, or at least a deviation from it, was necessary.

"You know, I've fought a lot of fires, but I think this will be the first time I've ever gone back into a burned building afterward."

"What's one of the strangest call outs you've ever had?"

They spent the next twenty minutes talking about the odd cases they'd seen. The conversation helped Leslie slowly relax as she pushed thoughts of the warehouse and the nightmares into the back of her mind. Once they finished eating, she gathered their plates and glasses and set them in the sink to wash later.

Clint's chair groaned as he pushed it away from the table and stood. When she turned, he was standing nearby, his eyes filled with compassion and concern.

"You don't have to go back to the warehouse." He reached out and gently took her hands in his. "Trust me. No one will think any less of you."

She knew he was right. Her colleagues would understand. Strangely enough, and for reasons she couldn't quite pin point, she was more worried about what Clint would think of her. "I appreciate that. I'm not going to lie—it's tempting to take you up on that and stay as far away from that place as possible." She looked down at their joined hands. A spark of awareness flared between them and pulsed straight to her heart. "If I don't do this, though, I'm afraid the nightmares are never going to end. Besides, I owe it to Danny. If going in there helps lead us to the man who shot him, then it'll be worth it."

Clint gently tugged her hands to bring her gaze back to his face. "Hey. I'm going to be right there with you the whole time."

"I'm glad, because I'm not sure I could do it without you."

He lifted one hand and softly brushed her chin with his thumb. "I like you, Leslie Granger. A lot." There was no missing the way admiration and heat tangled in his gaze.

His focus dropped to her lips, and it sent her heart racing.

"I like you, too, Clint Baker."

In one motion, he took a small step forward, leaned in, and gently covered her mouth with his in a kiss that was somehow the perfect combination of sweetness and intensity. When she reached out to press her palm against his chest to steady herself, his arm went around her waist, and he pulled her closer to deepen the kiss.

Leslie had no idea how long they stood there until a chime in the background slowly forced its way into her conscious thought. Clint must have heard it, too, because he broke the kiss, even though he didn't drop his arm.

"It's a notification on my phone. To remind me that it's time to leave for the warehouse."

She sounded breathless—a detail Clint must've liked because the corners of his mouth lifted in a smile.

"Then we'd better get going." He took his time pressing a kiss to the corner of her mouth before releasing her.

That amazing kiss she'd shared with Clint thoroughly occupied her mind until they drove through the gate and into the warehouse parking lot. As they approached the large building, her stomach cramped up, and she tried to ignore the wave of nausea that made her regret eating breakfast at all.

Her nightmare from last night pushed its way into her thoughts, and she had to remind herself that it wasn't real. They'd gotten Danny out of there in time, and he was at the hospital healing.

Even though they were ten minutes early, they certainly weren't the first to arrive. Detective Paris was speaking with four other officers near the grouping of police cars.

Another vehicle approached and parked beside Clint's and Chief Menendez got out. Clint and Leslie joined him.

The chief took a minute to look over the warehouse. One end of the building had collapsed on itself with pieces of debris littering the ground around it. The metal supports and sheeting were bent and twisted at odd angles and covered with soot. They wouldn't be able to go near that area once they got inside.

The rest of the building looked sound, though. They wouldn't have been given the green light to go back inside if that weren't the case. But she doubted the damage was repairable.

"They're going to need to tear the warehouse down and put up a new one," Chief Menendez observed. "I wonder how much of the stored paper was salvageable."

"Probably not much."

Even if the fire didn't touch the whole building, smoke would've done significant damage, not to mention water from the sprinklers overhead.

The chief opened the door and retrieved a pair of flashlights that he handed to Leslie. The electricity had been cut off as soon as the fire was discovered. It would be dangerous to restore it now. Much of the warehouse would be dark. The chief lifted a box of hard hats, which Clint took from him, and then closed the door.

They walked over to where Paris and the other officers were waiting. Once pleasantries were exchanged and the protective headgear handed out, the group approached an open door.

"The manager gave us access to the warehouse," Detective Paris explained. "He's nearby and said he'd check in with us again before we left. You all know what areas you're supposed to cover. We're looking for anything that the shooter might have left behind. Bullet casings, firefighter gear, or anything else that seems out of place."

Chief Menendez spoke up. "I got a call from the fire marshal last night. The investigators confirmed that kerosene was used to start the fire, and we all know this place is filled with enough paper to keep the fire going. The point of origin was at the southwest corner which means our arsonist has likely been all over this building."

Paris nodded. "He was either killed in the fire or he likely slipped out long before we had a police presence on the property. That said, we've learned to assume nothing. Keep your heads on a swivel and stick with your partners. We don't need any lone wolves here today. Report anything and everything you find."

They entered the building together. Once inside, Paris and Menendez discussed more aspects of the fire investigation as they moved off in one direction. The other four officers proceeded in pairs, leaving Clint and Leslie working as a team.

Clint took a flashlight from his belt and flicked it on.

Leslie did the same with the one the chief had given her. Light from outside the door illuminated the entrance, but what filtered in was quickly swallowed by the darkness ahead. Memories of going into the warehouse with Danny collided with those from the nightmare last night, and the combination made Leslie hesitate.

Clint reached over and gave her hand a gentle squeeze. "You've got this."

"Thank you." She squeezed back before they dropped their physical connection and focused on the job ahead of them.

"Do you remember what direction you and Danny went? If we can, we need to find the room where the shooting took place."

Everything looked different without smoke or the fire glowing in the distance.

"We were searching for potentially missing employees. We took the area over there." She shined her flashlight in the general direction. "We followed the hallways around to that far side of the building."

"Okay, let's start there."

Chapter Sixteen

lint gave Leslie enough space to lead as they slowly made their way down hallways and through rooms, scouring the area with their flashlights and looking for anything that stood out. The radio on his belt came to life occasionally as people reported in, and he did the same. So far, no one had found anything of importance in the last hour, but the warehouse they were searching was expansive. It could take some time to finish their investigation.

They went through a maze of hallways until they entered a larger area. Leslie, who had kept an even pace, suddenly stilled. She slowly looked around them as though she were trying to orient herself. Maybe even remember something. Clint waited silently, giving her the time she needed.

She glanced at him, and the haunted look in her eyes cut him to the core. In that moment, all he wanted to do was gather her in his arms and protect her from all of this. Memories of their kiss that morning made his need to shelter her even more intense.

"We saw the shooter for the first time here." She turned again and pointed her flashlight to the hallway on the right. "He was standing over there and waving his arms to get our attention. Keyes and Cho were working to get one of the employees out of the building. For a moment, I thought it might be one of them who needed help. It was impossible to identify him in the dim light and smoke. He looked like any other firefighter."

It made sense. The headlamps alone would make it difficult to see the man's face inside his helmet or even notice that the name badge was missing from his jacket. "What happened next?"

"I said something over the radio. I don't remember what —maybe asking if something was wrong. Danny must have thought it was Keyes or Cho, too, because he immediately went toward him. I followed."

Cautiously, she continued in that direction. The hallway ended with an open doorway on the right. Leslie stepped through it, shifted slightly to her left, and stopped. Clint moved to stand beside her.

"Here. This is where he shot Danny." Her flashlight illuminated several water jugs against one wall. "I remember seeing the water. I don't know why that stuck out. Maybe because of the fire." She motioned to the ceiling high above them. "The glow from the fire reflected off the metal."

Clint illuminated the room with his flashlight. A water cooler sat against the far wall along with a short counter that held a coffee maker and a microwave. A small table was set up in one corner. It was a breakroom, and the door they came in was the only way in or out of the room.

"When I came around the corner, Danny was over to the right, and the shooter was standing in the middle of the room with his gun aimed at him. As soon as I came in, Danny moved to stand between us." Her voice cracked. "I didn't see much after that. Danny tried to get him to calm down, and I heard the gun go off moments later."

Leslie lowered her flashlight to the floor where a reddish-brown stain marred the concrete. "He fell right there. I ran and dropped to his side. The shooter walked away. He didn't try to shoot me, and he didn't run. He walked out of the room as if he didn't have a care in the world." Her gaze slid from the spot to the wall across the room.

Clint placed a hand on the back of her neck, his thumb gently rubbing the tense muscles coiled beneath his hand. "You've done an amazing job." He picked up his radio and spoke into it. "Granger and I have located the site of the shooting. It's a breakroom about halfway down the building on the east side. Beginning to look for evidence now."

"Copy that."

He gave Leslie's shoulder a squeeze. "I'm going to take some pictures for evidence, and then we need to go through the room. See if we can find the casing from the bullet. We know this guy has been careful to wear gloves, but he may not have thought about it when he loaded the gun."

She looked at him, her eyes focused with determination. "If there's even a chance there could be a partial print on that casing, then we need to find it."

He nodded once and pointed his flashlight at one area of the room. "Given where the shooter was standing, it's most likely over there, although it could've rolled anywhere."

She began their search while he took pictures of the room from different angles followed by multiple pictures of the blood stain on the floor. He imagined Danny lying there and Leslie trying to figure out how to get him out of the warehouse before he bled out or the structure collapsed on top of them.

It was odd that the suspect hadn't gone on to shoot Leslie as soon as Danny fell. He also could've come back and picked her off like a sitting duck while she was tending to her partner. Either he wanted Leslie alive, Danny really was his primary target, or he was too concerned about getting out before the police arrived to care about anything else. Whatever the case, Clint sent up a silent prayer of thanks that she'd been spared.

His radio crackled to life. "This is Carrington. Smith and I found a storage closet. A bucket was turned upside down like a stool, and there are numerous empty water bottles and food wrappers on the floor. There's also a digital scanner. The battery is dead, but I'm willing to bet it was tuned into the fire station."

Paris's voice was next. "He got into the warehouse at some point then must have waited in the storage closet until most of the employees had left for the day. He started the fire. Maybe he came back to the closet again until he heard the fire department arrived?"

Had the shooter waited for most of the employees to leave because he'd wanted fewer people to be potentially injured in the fire? Or because there would be less people to spot him when he tried to make his escape?

Paris's theory was a sound one, but something didn't quite add up for Clint. "This guy has been meticulous about not leaving evidence, and yet he left all of that behind. It doesn't track." He continued to search for the casing as he listened to the radio conversation.

"Maybe he meant to come back and couldn't. Or he

thought it was all going to go up in flames and take care of the evidence for him," one of the other officers replied.

"Take pictures of absolutely everything and then bag it all," Paris ordered. "We'll take it back to the lab and go through it."

"Understood."

The radio went quiet again.

Clint looked across the room where Leslie was stooped as she looked for the casing beneath the table.

Sensing his gaze, she lifted her chin and paused. "Even if he wore gloves the whole time he was waiting and eating, there's still a chance the lab can find DNA, right?"

"Absolutely. On the rims of the water bottles if nothing else."

She gave a hopeful nod and went back to her search.

Clint had no doubt they'd find some DNA, but unless the shooter was already in the system, it wouldn't do them much good now. However, once they caught the guy, they could use the DNA to irrefutably put him at the scene of the crime.

"Hey, Clint? Check this out."

She'd shifted her search to the small cabinet that supported the coffee maker and microwave. She was shining her flashlight at the base, and that's when Clint realized it was on wheels.

He got down on the floor with her and looked beneath it. On the far side next to the wall was something shiny. It could certainly be a bronze casing.

"Awesome job, Leslie. Let me get a picture of this cabinet and its location, then we'll roll it out of the way and see what we've got."

They had to move the table and chairs in order to have enough room to shift the cabinet down. Once they did and got a closer look, there was no doubt it was the bullet casing they'd been searching for.

Clint got several photos showing where it'd been found, then some macro shots as well. When he was satisfied, he pulled a glove from his pocket, put it on, and got a plastic bag out of another pocket.

"Wow, you're prepared."

He smiled. "I do my best." With the opening of the bag on the floor next to the bronze casing, he used a gloves finger to gently nudge it inside then sealed the top. "There we go." Clint spoke into his radio, "Granger found the bullet casing. I've bagged it, and we're on our way out." He didn't see any reason for her to spend more time in the warehouse than she'd already had to endure.

"Nicely done." Paris sounded encouraged. "You and Granger head back to the entrance. All other teams should do the same once you've finished searching the room you're currently in."

"Understood." Clint clipped the radio back to his belt and put a hand against Leslie's back. "Come on. Let's get you out of here."

"Gladly."

He felt the slightest shiver in the muscles of her back as she leaned into his touch. She'd been an absolute trooper coming back here after all she'd been through. Now all he wanted was to get her out of the warehouse and back into the sunshine where she belonged.

Chapter Seventeen

Leslie tilted her face toward the sky and closed her eyes as she welcomed the warmth of the sun on her skin. She'd truly dreaded going back into that warehouse. But she did it, and they found the evidence they'd gone in for.

Clint had kept a hand against her back all the way back out of the warehouse. Now, he lightly bumped her arm with his. "Are you okay?"

"Better now." She lowered her chin and looked at him with a relieved smile.

"Good."

The other teams trickled out over the next five minutes until they were all standing together by the group of police cars. The warehouse manager returned and, with Detective Paris's blessing, closed the door and secured the building again.

Collectively, they made sure all evidence was documented before Paris dismissed the other two teams of officers leaving just him, Leslie, Clint, and Menendez.

"The lab will go through everything. I'm hoping they'll

be able to pull fingerprints and get DNA samples." Detective Paris leaned against the bumper of his car. "I'm reading through the list of call outs that you gave Officer Baker. Thank you for getting those to us, Chief."

"Absolutely. If there's anything else I can do, please let me know. I appreciate you keeping me updated." Menendez reached out and shook Paris's hand before he turned to Leslie. "If you need additional time off, please let me know. Given the circumstances, I'd be happy to grant the request."

As much as Leslie appreciated the offer, she couldn't fathom just sitting around her house waiting for news on the case. She'd much rather be at work doing something useful and keeping her mind occupied.

"Thank you, sir, but I'll be in for my shift tomorrow."

If Menendez disagreed with her decision, he kept his thoughts to himself.

"Excellent. I'll see you then." He gave her a nod, thanked the officers, and got into his car to leave.

Menendez seemed to be fine with her returning to work tomorrow, but she wasn't so sure Clint agreed with the surprised look he gave her.

The chief collected the flashlight from Leslie, loaded the hard hats into his car, and left.

Detective Paris addressed Clint. "Carrington and Smith are on their way to pick up Ortiz and bring him by the station. If we head back now, we should get there just in time to question him."

"Absolutely. I'll head that way momentarily."

Paris gave him a nod, thanked Leslie for her part in the warehouse search, and drove away.

Leslie turned to find Clint watching her closely.

"Taking a few days off before you go back to work isn't a bad idea."

She flashed a smile that she hoped would put him at ease. "Are you worried about me, Officer Baker?"

"Yes." He reached up and gently tucked a wayward section of hair behind one ear. "I want to keep you safe."

The gentle sincerity sent tendrils of warmth through her body until they settled in her chest.

"I know. But I can't just sit around waiting for something to happen. At least I'll stay busy and can do some good while I'm at work." She shrugged. "You and I aren't that different. I suspect, if our roles were reversed, you would do the same."

"You're not wrong." He sighed and gave her a wry grin. "I can drive you back to your house and make sure it's clear before I head to the station."

"I appreciate that, but could you drop me off at the hospital instead? I'd like to go and check on Danny and Becca. Visit a while and see if they need anything."

"Will you do me a favor and hang out there until we finish questioning Ortiz? I'll come find you. Between the security guards and one of our own watching over Danny, you should be safe there, but please don't hesitate to call me if something seems off." He reached over and covered her hand with his. "Keep your eyes open, okay?"

"I'll be careful."

Before going up to Danny's hospital room, Leslie stopped at the gift shop. She'd hoped to find something funny or cheerful to bring up for him. She'd nearly laughed out loud at one mug that was hilarious but probably not the most appropriate.

She finally settled on a bottle of Dr Pepper—his favorite soda—and a pair of humorous socks. They totally gave off a Dr. Mario vibe with the bright colors and little pills covering the main part of the socks. On the bottom of the right one, it read, "If you can read this..." and on the bottom of the left sock, it continued, "...give me the good meds."

Danny probably wouldn't wear them, but if it brought a smile to his face, then it would be worth it.

She browsed for something to get Becca then took everything she'd found to the counter to pay for them.

Even if she hadn't known where Danny's room was, it was easy to spot what with the officer standing outside. She didn't think she'd ever met this one, but when she gave her name, he ushered her inside with a smile.

Leslie entered hesitantly. "Hey, guys. You up for some company?"

"Hey, partner. Come on in." Danny pushed himself up a little higher in the bed. He reached over and used the remote control to mute the TV.

Becca, who was sitting nearby with a crochet project in her lap, placed everything in a canvas bag and stood to give Leslie a hug. "Thanks for coming by. We'd love some company."

Leslie smiled at her then walked over to the bed to give Danny's arm a squeeze. "How are you doing?"

He shrugged. "Honestly? I'm drained. I'm not sure I've ever been so tired in my life. And then I get tired of sleeping." He chuckled and immediately grimaced.

"Have you seen the doctor yet today?"

"No, not yet."

Becca reclaimed her seat. "The nurse said it'll likely be this evening." She pulled her crochet project back out of the bag and held it up. "With all the waiting around here, I just might have this baby blanket done by tomorrow."

The combination of dark green, lighter green, and brown looked really good together. "It's beautiful. Maybe the doctor will give you some good news when he does finally stop by."

"I sure hope so." Danny lowered his voice. "It's impossible to get much rest in the hospital. I'll probably recover quicker once I got home."

"No doubt." Except that, if the doctor wasn't ready to send him home, then it was for a good reason. "Well, I wanted to bring you a little something to brighten your day."

Leslie made a big show of fishing around in the small bag and pulled out the Dr Pepper. "I don't know if they're allowing soda or not, but I figured you could use the caffeine and sugar boost anyway."

Danny reached for the bottle. "Oh, it's even cold." With that, he twisted the cap off and took a long swig. "Thank you."

"Of course. But that's not all. I found something everyone in the hospital needs." The socks she'd purchased came in a small box similar to one a tie might be packaged in. It was nice because you could easily see what was written on the soles.

She handed them to him, and he immediately laughed with a groan and turned them around to show Becca. "You'll have to help me put these on later."

She grinned. "Definitely. Those are fabulous."

Leslie closed her hand around the third item in the bag.

"One last thing for you, Becca, because I figured you could probably use a little pampering." She handed over a pair of fuzzy rose-colored socks that, according to the tag, contained soothing aloe.

Becca ran her thumbs over the soft fabric. "Absolutely. So thoughtful of you. Thank you." She motioned to the chair on the other side of the room. "Bring that over and have a seat for a bit."

They talked about the cooler weather that was rolling in overnight, hospital food, and the lack of quality television shows.

Leslie was trying to think of a way to turn the conversation to an update on the case, but she needn't have worried because Danny brought it up first.

"Do you have any news on the investigation front?" He took another drink of his soda and put the lid back on.

"Actually, I do." She told them an abbreviated version about finding the casing, the possibility of getting DNA or fingerprints, and how Paris and Clint were probably questioning Ortiz right now. "With any luck, we'll have some answers soon."

"From your mouth to God's ears." Danny laid his head back on the pillow and closed his eyes for a moment. "Leslie, will you do me a favor?"

"Of course."

"Will you take my stubborn wife down to the cafeteria and make her buy some lunch? She needs to eat something else besides granola bars." He pinned his wife with a serious look.

Becca rolled her eyes. "I'm eating more than granola bars. I just feel bad bringing anything big in here when he's not up to eating much."

"Honey, I told you it won't bother me. I promise. I just need you to take good care of yourself and the baby. Okay?"

"How can you argue with that?" Leslie extended a hand to Becca who welcomed the assistance to stand. "I'll have her back soon."

"Good deal." Danny closed his eyes again, and Leslie was pretty sure he was asleep before they left the room.

The women chit chatted about the baby as they walked to the cafeteria. Becca was pleased to see they were offering sweet and sour chicken with rice so she had a bowl put together and even agreed to eat in the cafeteria so that Danny could get some rest.

Leslie chose a cup of chicken tortilla soup so that Becca wasn't eating alone.

Halfway through her meal, Becca set her fork down, her expression becoming serious.

"I'm worried about Danny. I know he's recovering and that's going to take a while, but he seems so tired today. More tired than he was yesterday evening even after coming out of surgery. I don't know, I can't explain it. His eyes don't look right." She sighed. "Maybe I'm just being paranoid."

Leslie reached across the table and gave her friend's hand a squeeze. "You know Danny better than anyone else here. Ask the doctor when he comes by. It doesn't hurt to be cautious, and that's a far cry from being paranoid."

She tried to distract Becca by asking about her baby shower, which Becca told her all about.

When she was done eating, they made their way back to Danny's hospital room where he was still sleeping soundly. With a whispered goodbye, she left so that he could rest and Becca could maintain her vigil.

Since she'd promised she'd wait for Clint, she decided

to claim a chair at the end of the hall from Danny's room and read for a while. Or at least try. Every time she made herself focus on the words, her mind either drifted back to Becca's worries, the kiss she'd shared with Clint, or the fact that the man who'd put Danny in the hospital was still out there somewhere.

Chapter Eighteen

Ortiz may have been a lot of things, but Clint had a hard time believing the man was capable of attempted murder. Especially since, from the moment he sat down in the interrogation room, he couldn't stop apologizing for all the things he'd stolen at the fire station.

"I never wanted to take them, but I had no control over it. I thought about putting them back, but I was afraid I'd get caught. That's why I threw most of it away. I certainly didn't deserve to keep them." Ortiz hung his head. "It was never my intention to hurt anyone I worked with."

Clint looked to his left where Dr. Gerard was sitting. The two of them were watching the interview from the other side of a one-way mirror. Only Detective Paris was in the room with their suspect. Dr. Gerard had thought Ortiz might be more likely to open up if he didn't feel as though he were being ganged up on.

"What have you been doing since you quit working for the fire department?" Paris had clearly thought through his line of questioning. By avoiding words like "fired," he was helping Ortiz feel more relaxed. Less judged.

Their suspect raked his fingers through his hair before pressing palms together and placing them between his knees. "I went to rehab for a while. Four months or so, maybe? It helped some. My doctor prescribed medication, and I've been working on some behavioral therapy. I think that's helped the most. I'm also going to support groups and doing my best not to relapse."

"That's great, Mr. Ortiz. I'm happy to hear that. Where do you work now?"

"I transcribe documents from home for a doctor's office here in town. On the weekend and evenings, I help a non-profit organization with their food pantry." For the first time since coming into the station, Ortiz looked engaged and excited as he spoke about his work. "Being able to provide food for people who might otherwise go hungry is a true privilege."

Paris nodded and offered a kind smile. "It sounds like a wonderful opportunity. You know, I only have a few more questions for you, but I could use some coffee. Can I get you a cup?"

"Please. Sugar if you have it."

"Absolutely. I'll be back in just a minute." Paris patted the table with his hand and stood.

Less than a minute later, the door to the observation room opened, and Paris slipped inside.

"Thoughts, Dr. Gerard?"

"He seems to genuinely regret what's happened in the past. The combination of medication and behavioral therapy coupled with a support group seems to be doing a world of good to keep his kleptomania under control. By making a living transcribing medical records, he's removing the general temptation to steal that he might face by working outside the home. Spending his free time helping others in need keeps him from getting bored and helps put a focus on others." Gerard motioned to the man sitting patiently in the interrogation room. "I see nothing in his behavior to suggest he's the man you're looking for."

Paris nodded thoughtfully. "I was thinking that as well. I want to ask him about taking the turnout gear and the man he seemed to be working with that day. Do you see any reason why I shouldn't?"

"Avoid making it sound like an accusation, or he could become agitated and withdraw."

Clint leaned forward and rested his elbows on his knees. "If stealing something like the gear is not common for someone with kleptomania, then Ortiz was likely very uncomfortable taking it in the first place. It could be that the man who was helping him orchestrated the theft."

"All right. I'm going to grab us both some coffee and head in for round two." Paris left the room and closed the door quietly behind him.

"I've never known someone with kleptomania," Curtis said conversationally. "It sounds like it's not unlike alcoholism or drug use."

"You're right. It's an addiction that hurts him as much or more than it does the people he steals from. There's a lot of shame and embarrassment associated with the illness, and it's difficult to ask for help. The fact that Ortiz has done so much to better his condition and his life speaks volumes about his character. He can't help having kleptomania, but he's doing everything he can to thrive in spite of it."

Yeah, there was no way this guy was targeting firefighters and trying to kill them. If it hadn't been for his illness rearing its ugly head, Ortiz likely would've been a valuable addition to the Destiny Fire Department.

Paris entered the interrogation room again, this time with two cups of coffee in paper cups. He set one in front of Ortiz, gave him three packets of sugar and a coffee stirrer, then took a seat.

"Look, Ortiz, the main reason I needed you to come in is because I need your help locating someone. There's a man in Destiny who started a dangerous fire and was seen wearing a set of gear stolen from one of the fire stations."

The other man had been adding the packets of sugar into his coffee and stirring it, but at the mention of stolen gear, he set the cup back down on the table with a shaky hand. "I don't know anything about that."

"I'm not suggesting that you do. But my understanding is that, right before you quit your job as a firefighter, you'd considered taking a set of turnout gear."

Ortiz sat up straighter. "I returned that gear and apologized to the chief. It was never something I wanted to do."

"I believe that, and so does Chief Menendez. We know there was someone else at the station that day. A man that we suspect may have asked you to take the turnout gear. What can you tell me about him?"

Ortiz stared at the table for several moments before taking a sip of his coffee. "I was splitting the cost of renting an apartment with this other guy. He figured out about my kleptomania when I kept showing up at home with things I'd taken from the station." His eyes echoed the sadness and regret he'd likely always struggle to let go of. "He told me that if I didn't get him a set of turnout gear, then he'd go to the chief and tell him about my illness."

"You didn't want to lose your job."

The other man shook his head. "And I couldn't afford for him to move out and leave me with the full cost of rent. I figured no one would miss it, he'd stop asking, and that would be the end of it." He wrapped both hands around the cup. "You have to understand, I wasn't doing well back then. I know now that it only would've been the beginning. He would've kept asking me to take things. Getting caught meant the end of my dream career, but I'm glad it happened that way. I never would've gotten the help I needed if it hadn't."

Clint could tell the guy was genuine, but it was also clear that he was leaving the name of his roommate out on purpose. Combine that omission with the way he was picking at the edge of his paper cup, and he was clearly getting uncomfortable.

Paris took a drink of his own coffee and leaned forward in a way that made his questions seem more conversational. "The man we're looking for now shot a firefighter, and he's still threatening others. We need to find him and stop him before he hurts anyone else. There are some parallels between our suspect and your old roommate. It would be a huge help if you could give me his name. If it's not him, then we'll rule him out and be on our way. But if it is, you could be saving lives."

"Look, I want to help you. Trust me, I do. But I need your promise that you won't say a word about me to him. I don't want him to know I'm involved whether he's your guy or not."

"You have my word. Your name will never come up." Paris stretched out his hand.

Ortiz studied him a moment before clasping the detective's hand and giving it a shake. "His name was Rick Castor. I'm going to warn you, though, I'm not so sure that's his real name. I once heard an acquaintance of his call him Jake. I never knew for sure either way."

"That's a huge help, Domingo, thank you. Could you describe Rick for me?"

Ortiz leaned back into his chair for the first time since he'd stepped foot in the interrogation room. Clint could only assume that being able to help Detective Paris had finally put him at ease.

"He was about my height—five eight. Brown hair, brown eyes. Really, he was just your average guy. No tattoos or scars that I ever noticed."

"Do you happen to know where he is now?"

Ortiz shook his head. "No. He'd moved out of the apartment completely by the time I got back there that same night. I ended up having to move myself within a month. I haven't seen him since that night at the fire station."

"All right. Thanks again, Mr. Ortiz. I truly appreciate your time. If you'll give me just a moment, I'll find Officer Carrington and have him take you home."

Ortiz was escorted out of the station, and Detective Paris thanked Dr. Gerard for his expertise. The detective turned to Clint. "I'm going to have IT do a search for Rick Castor and cross reference that name with the list of call outs that Chief Menendez gave us. See if we can't get a hit."

"That sounds like a good plan." Clint checked his watch. It was nearly one o'clock. He really wanted to get over to the hospital and check on Leslie. Besides, if she was even half as hungry as he was, they both needed to get something to eat. "I'd like to stick close to Leslie this afternoon. Between going to the warehouse and speaking with Ortiz, we may be dangerously close to disturbing the wasp's nest."

"Agreed. I spoke with Chief Dolman earlier. You've

worked a lot of extra hours lately. Don't worry about coming back to the station until tomorrow."

Knowing that he wouldn't have to leave Leslie's side for the rest of the day made him feel a whole lot better. They may have gotten a slew of potential information about the shooter today, and hopefully it would eventually lead to an ID and an arrest. With any luck, they could wrap this up soon.

For now, though, Leslie was still in danger. For all they knew, the shooter could be right under their noses.

Clint had just dropped something off at his desk and was writing something down on his calendar when a shadow fell over his desk. He looked up to find Officer Mari Smith with a tense look on her face.

"I'm sorry to interrupt. We just got a call into dispatch. One of Leslie Granger's neighbors heard a commotion out on the street in front of her house and called it in. A patrol responded immediately from a block over. When they arrived, they found someone had taken a baseball bat to Leslie's car window and left something inside."

Detective Paris's jaw tightened. "I'm heading over there now."

"Leslie's at the hospital visiting Bracken. I'll pick her up, and we'll be there as soon as possible."

Worry tightened around Clint's chest like a vice. He couldn't believe this guy smashed Leslie's car in broad daylight. He was either getting bolder or becoming desperate.

Neither was a good thing.

Chapter Nineteen

First someone broke into her home and now her car. Clint said something had been left inside. Leslie had no idea what to expect when she saw it. Whoever did this was bold enough to come back to her house and vandalize her car during the day knowing that officers were patrolling the area more than normal. It was a scary realization.

"Hey." Clint's voice broke the silence and startled Leslie. She'd been clutching the strap of her bag in her left hand so hard that it was beginning to ache. He reached past the computer and took her hand, slipping his fingers between hers. "Everything will be okay. This guy is going to mess up, and when he does, we'll be right there to catch him."

She nodded and prayed he was right.

He squeezed her hand then gripped the steering wheel as he turned onto her street and pulled to a stop just down from her car.

She released her seatbelt, but Clint's words stopped her.

"It's starting to get cold outside. Do me a favor and stay

here where it's warm. Let me see what's in your car first. That way I can give you some warning. I promise I'll come right back."

"Yeah. That's a good idea." She refused to allow herself to go over the possibilities as she watched him approach her car, speak with another officer, and finally peer through the busted window. It looked like he might've taken pictures with his phone.

Another officer leaned into the car with a camera to capture official pictures of the evidence.

As she waited, she scanned the street and her neighbors' homes. One family was out on the front porch watching all the excitement. She caught sight of someone else's outline as they watched through their living room window. Between this and her house, there'd been more excitement on this street in the last two days than the last two years combined. Officers were already heading out to knock on doors to gather statements and look for witnesses.

It seemed like an eternity before Clint finally walked back toward his car and sat behind the wheel.

"What kind of damage am I looking at? Please tell me he didn't leave anything gruesome." At this point, the one thing their suspect had proven was that he was unpredictable.

"It's just the one window that was smashed. Nothing looks damaged inside. And no, it's nothing like that. He left a melted child's toy in the driver's seat. I can show you pictures..."

"No. I need to see it for myself."

Clint didn't look the least bit surprised. He walked around the car and opened her door.

The instant she was out, she felt his protective hand settle on her back. Its warmth permeated her jacket and shirt, a silent transfer of strength as he escorted her toward the shattered window.

An officer stepped back and gave her a nod. Leslie leaned forward, careful not to touch the door, and gasped.

A toy fire truck sat on the driver's seat. It looked like it was crafted from a combination of plastic and metal. Someone must have set it into the middle of a fire because parts of the front of the truck and the ladder drooped where the plastic melted and ran. The tires had melted as well, and most of the sides were blackened.

The only part of the truck that hadn't been touched by heat or flame was a piece of paper taped to the ladder. Written in black marker was the word, GRANGER.

Detective Paris approached. "It doesn't look like the seat was damaged, which means the truck was melted else-where and brought here afterward. He could have easily broken the window and thrown something inside to torch your car. Instead, he'd wanted to send a message." He turned and addressed a nearby officer. "We need to process that truck as soon as possible. Focus on the note. It looks handwritten. I want to know immediately if you find anything."

A touch to her arm drew Leslie's attention to Clint.

"Come on. Let's get you inside. This could take a while, and there's no need for you to stand out here in the cold and wait."

She rubbed her arms in an unsuccessful attempt to warm up and allowed him to guide her up the walkway to her house. Somehow, she was able to fish out her keys and unlock the door. Apparently, the unsteady range of emotions didn't translate to her hands.

Leslie switched on the living room lights and waited for Clint to scan the house to make sure everything was secure.

A minute or two later they were in the kitchen. Red and blue lights from the police cars outside came through the blinds and painted colors on the walls.

Her adrenaline was still pumping, and she couldn't seem to stop moving. Needing to feel useful, she put a saucepan of milk on the stove and started heating it up.

"Would you like a cup of hot chocolate?" It was all she could think of to do.

"That's a great idea. I'd love some, thank you."

She was aware of him watching her as she took out two mugs, found the cocoa mix in her pantry, and pulled a spoon from the silverware drawer. She measured out the right amount of powder for each mug.

Leslie went to stir the milk when she was stopped by Clint's hand on her arm. "I'm okay."

"I know you are, but I'm worried about you. You've been through a lot of stress over the last couple of days. It'd be enough to push anyone past their breaking point."

She filled the mugs with hot milk then set the pitcher on a burner. Methodically, she mixed the first cup and handed it over to Clint before mixing the other. The spoon clanged against the bottom of the sink where she dropped it to be washed later.

Leslie claimed a spot on the couch, and she was both surprised and pleased when Clint sat beside her. Without hesitation, he put an arm around her shoulders. She leaned into his side.

Together, they sipped their hot chocolate in silence. The sound of doors slamming and distant voices outside periodically interrupted their bubble of peace.

Leslie could picture Mr. Moody two houses down griping about how the neighborhood was going to pot. If anyone had seen something, it likely would've been him. In fact, she wouldn't be the least surprised if he was the one who called it in to the police in the first place.

"Security cameras." The words left her mouth before she realized she was going to say them. "I think I'm going to get some security cameras after payday. I mean, investing that money pretty much guarantees I won't need them, right?" She could certainly hope that was the case.

"I think one for each door would be a good idea." He took another sip from his mug and rested his cheek against the side of her head. "This is some of the best hot chocolate I've ever had."

"I won a canister of it in a white elephant gift exchange at the station last Christmas. I've been hooked on it ever since. It's hard to find during the summer, so I'm planning to stock up this winter, so I'll be set for next year."

She reached over and set her mug on the coffee table. When she returned to her spot by Clint's side, she rested a hand against his chest. The steady rhythm of his heart sent a wave of peace through her. It was scary how quickly she was coming to rely on this amazing man who was dangerously close to capturing her heart.

"You'll have to text me the name so I can get some for my parents. It'd make a good addition to their Christmas gifts."

"I'll take a picture of the canister for you."

Clint shifted to place his mug next to hers. "Sounds like a plan." He placed a hand over hers and softly stroked the backs of her fingers with his thumb.

When she tilted her head to look up at him, he was watching her with a longing that stole her breath. The last of the chill from being outside fled as he kissed her. His lips explored hers slowly, thoroughly, coaxing a sigh of contentment.

A knock at the door splintered their perfect moment of peace. Clint broke the kiss but pressed another to her forehead before standing and going to the door.

He greeted someone then stepped aside so that they could enter.

Detective Paris stood in the center of the room and addressed Leslie. "I knew you'd want an update. Your car has been dusted for prints, and we've taped plastic over your window just in case it rains. You'll want to call your insurance company tomorrow to have that window replaced. We're taking the toy fire truck back to the precinct with us. With any luck, there'll be some evidence left behind. Even finding out what kind of fire melted the plastic could give us a push in the right direction."

Clint nodded. "That's good. What about the neighbors? Someone called it in. Did anyone see anything?"

Smashing the glass out of a car window had to have made some noise. Surely someone heard that and looked out the window.

"Two different neighbors reported seeing a man in a dark jacket with the hood pulled low over his head. He had what looked like a baseball bat, and that's what he used to break the window. Neither of them saw his face or a car on the street that didn't belong there. Once he busted out the window and set something inside, he took off running south and cut across someone's back lawn. That's where we lost track of him."

Disappointment coiled itself in Leslie's chest. "This guy's like a ghost. He keeps disappearing."

"He's also getting bolder," Clint added. "He obviously thinks he can avoid getting caught. I think he likes the challenge."

Leslie stood and reached for a section of hair and

absently coiled it around one of her fingers. Yes, the guy did seem to like the challenge. At this point, she was pretty confident that she was the target. Was it a matter of disrupting her life and frightening her? Or did he have a bigger agenda in mind? Assuming this was the same man who shot Danny, he was clearly capable of escalating.

Detective Paris agreed with Clint. "He's overconfident, and he probably thinks he's in control. That means he's more likely to make a mistake. The moment he does, we'll be there. Tomorrow, we're going to track down Ortiz's old roommate and find out what he knows. It's time we got some answers." He focused on Leslie, his concern evident. "Someone will be stationed within view of your house until we find this guy. I'm sorry for all you're going through, Leslie."

"Thank you."

It did make her feel a little better knowing that an officer would be nearby. Still, she had no idea how she was supposed to relax enough to fall asleep tonight. Not when every creak was going to make her wonder if someone was prowling around in the shadows. At the very least, she'd be keeping all the lights on. Her vision swam as unwanted tears flooded her eyes. She blinked them away. There wasn't time to fall apart.

Clint walked the detective out. They exchanged a few words before he closed the door again and secured the locks. He'd just turned around when her cell phone pinged.

The moment Becca's name appeared, Leslie's stomach dropped. Even as she swiped to read the text message, she knew it wasn't going to be good news.

> Please continue to keep Danny in your
> prayers. He's developed a fever, and the
> doctor says he's got an infection from the
> bullet wound or surgery. They're starting
> antibiotics.

"What's wrong?"

The kindness in Clint's voice in combination with the text had Leslie fighting for control over her emotions. Today had been one hit after another, and she wasn't sure how much more of this she could take.

Chapter Twenty

Worry sparked as Leslie handed over the phone and Clint read the text. Getting an infection this early in the recovery process could set Danny back and make it hard for his wounds to heal. At least the doctors at Destiny Community Hospital were some of the best. They'd stay on top of things and do what they could to help Danny. He moved to hand the phone back to Leslie and stopped.

She was staring at the wall behind him, her shoulders slightly rounded, her jaw clenched. Her chin quivered as a single tear squeezed past her defenses and rolled down her cheek.

Clint didn't ask for permission or worry that he was crossing a line. He simply tossed her phone onto the nearby couch and stepped forward to wrap his arms around her.

She leaned into his chest and buried her face in his shirt. If it weren't for the gentle shake of her shoulders and the occasional sniff, he wouldn't even know she was crying.

At first, he said nothing. All the platitudes in the world

wouldn't help ease the overwhelming stress and worry she had to be feeling right now.

It was only after her tears had subsided that he finally uttered the prayer in his heart.

"Dear Heavenly Father, we lift Danny up to You. Please hold him in Your mighty hand. Help his body to combat this infection and to heal the way you designed it to. Guide the doctors and nurses caring for him. Give Danny and Becca a healthy dose of peace, and let them feel Your presence in all things. We thank You that Danny's fellow firefighters were able to get him out in time, for the swift action of Curtis and the EMTs, and for a successful surgery that's brought him to where he is now."

Leslie swiped at the tears on her face and gave a gentle nod. "Yes, Lord," she breathed.

Clint rested his cheek against the side of her head. "I also pray a hedge of protection around Leslie. Please keep her safe. Not just physically. Guard her heart and her mind against any doubts and fear. Help us to figure out who's doing these terrible things so we can work together to bring justice for Danny and make sure no one else gets hurt. We are so thankful for Your many blessings, Father. Amen."

"Amen." Leslie slipped her arms around his waist and gave him a fierce hug.

He breathed in the subtle scent of her hair that reminded him of fresh flowers right after a spring rain.

She stepped away. Her eyes looked tired, and her cheeks were pink. Whether it was from crying or their hug, he wasn't sure. Most likely a combination.

"Thank you."

"For what?"

"Letting me fall apart like that. For not allowing me to do it alone."

"I just witnessed an amazingly strong woman completely shake off the past two days of stress and emerge even more resilient than ever." He reached out and lightly touched her cheek with his thumb. "You've got this."

"No. *We've* got this."

Something passed between them. It was fleeting and fragile and new, but it was there, and Clint prayed they'd get a chance to explore the possibilities together.

Leslie pressed her hands to her cheeks and gave a nervous laugh. "I'm going to go clean up. I feel like a mess."

"Take your time. I'll be here."

With a nod and a small smile, she turned and left the room.

Clint checked his watch. It was nearly four o'clock. As soon as he and Paris saw the melted fire truck in the driver's seat of Leslie's car, they knew things had escalated. Unlike breaking into the house and sending her a picture, torching a toy fire truck and attaching her name to it landed directly in the threat category. It still wasn't clear why the suspect was targeting her, though.

Before Clint had a chance to say anything earlier, Paris had expressed concern about Leslie staying at the house alone. It only echoed his own worries.

When she got back from cleaning up, he planned to offer to sleep on her couch. At least then he could watch her back. If she didn't agree, he'd stay in his car out front overnight.

He settled on the recliner and went through his e-mails and messages.

Twenty minutes later, Leslie walked back into the living room. Her hair, which she'd braided, was still wet and dripping a little onto the back of her shirt. She'd changed into an oversized long-sleeved shirt and a pair of lounge pants.

The biggest difference, however, was that she seemed more herself again. Her back was straight, her arms relaxed. Even though she had to be exhausted, she looked like she was ready to dive right back into the case. He greatly admired that about her.

Clint got to his feet and waited until she'd taken a seat on the couch before joining her.

"Thank you for waiting. Just the thought of showering while I was alone in the house gave me flashbacks of horror movie and bathroom murder scene I've ever seen." She shuddered.

He laughed. "Seriously, it wasn't a problem."

"Thanks for what you said earlier, too. I hate being that stereotypical woman who starts crying when things get rough."

He immediately raised a hand to stop her from continuing her train of thought.

"I'm going to share something my mom once told me. It was back in junior high. I was twelve and sure I knew everything. Well, I had a best friend named Ben, and we hung out all the time. Until one day, he betrayed my confidence. I'm not going to go into details, but I truly felt as though he'd stabbed me in the back."

It'd been like torture trying to get through the rest of the school day while Ben was laughing at him with some of the other kids.

"When I got home, I went right to my bedroom. And there I was, this big, macho preteen crying my eyes out. My mom came in, and I remember standing up and trying to wipe the tears away before she saw because I didn't want her to think I was being a baby." He shifted so he was facing Leslie. "Mom told me that sometimes crying is the body's way of getting rid of all those things that are weighing us down. Tears aren't simply drops of saltwater, they represent our worries and hurts and fears. We have to let them go before we're able to focus on something better."

"Wow." She swallowed hard and blinked tears from her eyes. "Your mom is good."

He laughed. "Yes, she is. Of course, this is the same woman who once yelled at me to clean my room, or she was going to buy a pig to complete the ensemble. So, there you go."

Leslie tipped her head back and laughed loudly, and he couldn't help but join in. It felt good to simply relax and share a laid-back moment with her.

And it was good to see that smile again, too.

His parents would like her. A lot. He prayed he'd have the opportunity to introduce her to them some day.

Clint's stomach growled, and he realized he never did eat lunch. Neither did Leslie. He'd planned to ask her out to eat before everything imploded this afternoon. "Why don't I call and have a pizza delivered?"

"What about work? Don't you need to go back to the precinct?"

Clint leaned forward a little. "I'm not going anywhere. After everything that happened with your car, I really don't feel comfortable leaving you here alone. I can crash on the couch tonight. Or if you'd prefer, I can stay in my car outside—it wouldn't be the first time. If you have no objections, of course."

He'd been prepared to give reasons why it would be a good idea. To his surprise, her uncertain expression gave way to relief as she nodded her agreement.

"I'd feel so much better if you stayed. I've got blankets and an extra pillow." She got to her feet.

"Are you sure it won't be an inconvenience?"

"I think I'm the one who should be asking *you* that."

He assured her that it wasn't, and some of the stress in her features seemed to melt away.

"Then I think a pizza is a great idea."

Clint placed the order online and joined Leslie in the kitchen where she was pulling down plates for their meal.

She turned to look at him. "Did anything come of the appointment with the psychologist? Is it possible that Ortiz is the person behind all of this?"

That's right, they hadn't even had a chance to talk about the interview.

"Dr. Gerard never met Ortiz, and he didn't have access to the files from Ortiz's stay at rehab. He did verify that much of Ortiz's behavior at the station sounded like klepto-mania except when he was caught trying to take the turnout gear. Apparently stealing something to sell or even working with someone else is very uncharacteristic of the illness."

"They never caught or identified the person who was helping Ortiz, did they?"

"Not at the time. He and Ortiz were roommates for a while." He told her a little more of what was said during the interview. "Ortiz did give us a name, but he hadn't seen the guy in over a year. Paris is hoping to track him down and bring him in for questioning tomorrow."

"You don't think it's Ortiz, do you?"

"Honestly? No. He's made mistakes, that's for sure. But there was nothing about the man that hinted at him being a stalker or becoming violent. His old roommate, though? That remains to be seen."

Leslie leaned against the counter and frowned. "I just

wish we knew why this was happening at all. I mean, if he *is* targeting me, there must be a reason. I keep wondering what I could've done to make someone hate me so much."

Clint couldn't imagine Leslie doing anything to make someone truly angry with her. Certainly not like this. He moved to stand in front of her and reached out to cup her elbows with his hands. "Whatever's going on, it has more to do with him than it does with you. Assuming you're the actual target. It could be a general anger toward the fire department, and something happened to put you and Danny on his radar."

"I'm tired of all the guess work, Clint."

He was, too. Not having solid answers was making it incredibly difficult to predict—and catch—the man responsible.

Clint excused himself to grab a duffel bag from his patrol car. He always carried it with him in case he needed a change of clothes when he was out late or on a stake-out. He even included personal items like a toothbrush and deodorant. He happily changed out of his uniform and into a regular pair of jeans and a long-sleeved shirt.

Once the pizza arrived, they spent the evening eating and watching a funny movie they'd both seen before. The predictable plot and laughs were exactly what they needed.

It was after ten when Leslie covered a yawn at the same time Clint stifled one of his own. They both chuckled at the timing.

Leslie ran a finger under one of her eyes. "As much as I don't want to admit it, I'm going to need to crash. Let me go get the pillow and blankets for you." She turned and went to the cabinet at the end of the hall. When she came back, her arms were full of blankets with a pillow balanced on top.

"This couch is actually really comfortable." She waited for him to move then started to arrange the bedding.

"Do you sleep out here often?"

She shrugged. "Sometimes. I did last night."

She likely slept on the couch when she had trouble falling asleep, and there was no wonder why she might not have gotten much rest with everything going on.

They worked together in silence as Clint helped her straighten the bottom blanket and then spread out another one on top.

Leslie tossed the pillow onto one end of the couch. She yawned again and groaned.

He gently cradled her face with his hands. "Go get some sleep. I've got everything under control out here."

"Promise you'll wake me up if any new information comes in?"

"I promise." He brushed a feather-light kiss against her lips before stepping back again. "Good night."

A soft pink dusted her cheeks. "Good night."

He waited until she'd walked down the short hallway and gone into her bedroom before he let himself flop back onto the couch.

Chapter Twenty-One

L eslie tossed the last bite of toast in her mouth and put the plate in the sink. She'd slept better last night than she had in days. Maybe part of it was because the body could only carry on so long on stress and chocolate. She wasn't naïve, though. She knew it was mostly because Clint had been sleeping in the living room. Knowing he was out there, and that she wasn't alone, was enough to put her completely at ease.

They'd both spent the morning bustling around her house getting ready for the day. He touched base with his brother. She called Cindy to see how the girls were doing. They'd fixed a simple breakfast of scrambled eggs and toast that was wolfed down in record time.

Clint ended his call and gave her an apologetic smile. "I had no idea that would take so long. We're trying to get things planned for our parents' anniversary in the spring. We were hoping for a cruise to Alaska. They've always talked about going."

"Wow, that's amazing. Are they going to be completely

surprised, or do you guys normally get them larger gifts like that?"

He laughed, and she loved the way the sound filled her kitchen. "We've never done anything like this before. I think they'll be completely shocked. But it's their fortieth anniversary, and we wanted to do something special."

"Well, I'm sure they're going to love it."

Leslie opened her large backpack to make sure she had everything she needed for her twenty-four hour shift. She always kept some necessities in her locker there, but the clothing she took back and forth as well as any specific snacks she wanted to have on hand.

When she looked up, she caught Clint watching her, his expression somewhere between worry and admiration. She immediately knew what he was thinking about.

She finished zipping the backpack closed. "I can't sit around here all day just doing nothing. Waiting for news about Danny or the case is slowly driving me insane."

"I know." He took several strides forward until they were toe-to-toe. He slid his fingers into her hair at the base of her neck, sending shivers racing down her spine. "Promise me you'll be careful."

"I promise..."

Her words, spoken barely above a whisper, were cut off when he kissed her with an intensity that had her grasping the fabric on the front of his uniform with one hand to steady herself. He poured his worries along with a myriad of unspoken promises into the brief kiss that left her catching her breath when he pulled back.

Leslie's mind swirled with questions and uncertainties, but the affection and heat in his gaze quieted them all. They had a lot of things to figure out—about the case and what was going on between them—and they would. But this morning wasn't the time.

"We'd better get going, or we're both going to be late." His voice was gruff as he reached for her backpack with one hand and lifted his duffel bag with the other.

They got everything loaded into his squad car and headed for station two.

"If I get any updates on the evidence, or if we can speak with Ortiz's old roommate, I'll let you know. I'm hoping we can get some answers today. Goodness knows we're due for them." Clint stopped at a red light and turned his head to look at her. "It's going to be weird to not see you for a full twenty-four hours. Especially after spending so much time together the last couple of days."

"You could come eat dinner with us." As soon as she extended the offer, she second-guessed herself. Not because she didn't want him to, but because it wouldn't come without a price.

"Wow, that sounded convincing." He hiked an eyebrow but was forced to change his focus back to the road when the light turned green.

Leslie groaned. "Sorry. I would really like for you to come eat dinner with us at the station. It's not unusual—friends and family drop by all the time. If you do, though, I guarantee there's going to be some teasing from the crew."

"They'll be teasing me or you?"

"Yes."

Clint laughed. "Well, that's good to know. Would that bother you?" He hazarded a quick glance in her direction.

"No. It wouldn't." Because she truly didn't care if her co-workers thought she and Clint were together. They kinda were, even if it wasn't official. At least she thought they were.

She found herself holding her breath as she waited for Clint's reaction.

"Then Then it doesn't bother me either. I'll do my best to be there. What time do you all usually eat?"

"Six. It's Bryce's turn to cook, too, which means you're in luck since it almost always involves barbecued meat of some kind."

That brought an appreciative smile to Clint's face. "Then I'll definitely be there." He winked at her. "I'll touch base around five and let you know for sure. But barring a lead or complication with the case, you can count me in."

He pulled into the parking lot of the fire department and slowed to a stop. "Remember, reach out if you need anything."

"I will." Tears pricked her eyes, which was super annoying because she was going to see him later that evening. She swallowed hard and blinked them away before he noticed.

They both got out, and he popped the truck so she could grab her backpack. With a final wave, she went inside to start her shift.

Clint studied the whiteboard that'd been set up in the conference room. They had a timeline written out starting with the attempted theft of the turnout gear two years ago, the missing retired gear nearly a year ago, all the way up to last night when someone broke into Leslie's car and left that threat.

The problem was, they had a lot of information, and very little of it fit together. They were missing a bit piece of the puzzle, and possibly more than one at that.

Detective Paris led the morning's update on the case, and even Chief Dolman was in attendance. It wasn't that unusual, but more than ever before, it was evident that all hands were on deck.

Paris pointed to Logan Alcott, the precinct's IT specialist. "Where are we in locating Rick Castor, the man who rented the apartment with Domingo Ortiz?"

"I found no record of a Rick Castor in Destiny. I searched for Richard Castor and Patrick Castor as well but came up empty. I tracked down the apartment that Ortiz was renting. Turns out, he was the only official renter on the lease. I spoke with Ortiz, and Rick paid him in cash, and it was Ortiz who wrote the monthly check to the landlord. As far as the apartment complex goes, there never was a Rick Castor." Logan leaned forward and looked at the laptop sitting on the table in front of him. "Ortiz mentioned he heard someone refer to Castor as Jake. But you'd be surprised how many Jakes and Jacobs there are in Destiny. Without a last name, I'm not sure how much luck we're going to have. I'm going to keep trying to find a connection, though."

Paris acknowledged his report and turned his attention to Officer Josh Carrington. "Did we hear back from the lab concerning the casing found at the scene of the shooting or the bucket and digital scanner found at the warehouse?"

Carrington stood and raked his fingers through his brown hair that always looked like he needed a trim. "Yes, the lab did find a partial fingerprint on the casing. It was enough to run through our database, but we didn't get a hit."

"That's rather unusual." Paris frowned. "Most criminals don't go from no offenses straight to attempted murder."

"Agreed. As for the bucket," Carrington continued, "there were multiple sets of fingerprints obtained, which tracks since we found it in a janitorial closet. However, there was only one set of fingerprints on the digital scanner that was also on the bucket. They belong to Christopher King. He works security at the warehouse and was there the night of the fire."

"Wait a minute." Clint held up a finger to interject. "Wasn't Leslie Granger's company sent in to look for two potentially missing employees? I thought one was named Chris."

"You're absolutely right." Carrington nodded to Logan who brought up a picture on this computer, which was connected to the TV in the conference room. "This is Christopher King. Firefighters Keyes and Cho eventually located him on the other side of the warehouse from the closet where the bucket and scanner were found. And as expected, the scanner was tuned to listen in on the fire department's communications."

Now they were finally getting somewhere. After all the dead ends they'd been hitting, at least this was something. Clint prayed it would lead them in the right direction.

"Nicely done," Chief Dolman spoke up from the far end of the table. "I want King brought in for questioning as soon as we're done here. Logan, what do we know about him?"

Logan pointed to the TV where King's picture was still up. "Christopher King was born in Alabama and moved to Texas with his family when he was fifteen years old. He graduated high school and got his first job as a security guard at a local pawn shop. Eventually, he got his first job as a security guard there. He started working for the paper company at the warehouse two years ago. Of course, being in security, his prints are on file."

"He has no priors," Carrington added.

"Pull his financial information," Paris instructed. "I want to know everything we can about this guy." He looked over at Clint. "Baker, do we have any updates on firefighters Bracken and Granger?"

"As of last night, Bracken is fighting an infection. The doctors are treating him with antibiotics, which will hopefully be enough to re-stabilize his condition. Granger's insurance company is supposed to send someone today to replace the window in her car. She's on shift until eight tomorrow morning, but I'll be touching base with her this evening. If she runs into any trouble, she knows to contact me or the precinct."

"Is there anything else?" When no one replied, Paris put his hands on the table and stood. "Then let's find King and hopefully get some answers."

Chapter Twenty-Two

Everyone at the station greeted Leslie with hugs and smiles. They asked if she was doing okay and wanted to know if she'd heard from Danny or Becca yet that morning. It was good to be back. At the same time, being there without Danny didn't feel right, especially since she hadn't heard from Becca since the text the night before. Even though everyone went about business as usual, the general energy of the station felt muted.

Leslie spent her morning cleaning her gear and checking every inch of it after the warehouse fire. It was more of a formality because Bryce had been kind enough to come back that night and wash out any trace of Danny's blood. She was thankful because she didn't think she could've made it through that and kept her composure. Still, even though she knew Bryce would've cleaned her gear, she went over it again anyway for something to focus on.

After that, she and Bryce went over the ladder truck from front to back, inside and out. Even though it wasn't unusual to work with him, she had a feeling he, or other co-workers, were sticking close to keep an eye on her. In fact, with the exception of a trip to the bathroom, she hadn't been more than five or six feet from someone since she'd arrived.

"I know what you're doing, Bryce. You and the others. I appreciate it, but I'm okay."

"I don't doubt that. But there's someone out there who has it out for you, and maybe firefighters at this station in general. We talked about it before you came back, and the chief agreed. No one is going to be on their own until this case gets wrapped up. Since your partner isn't here right now, the rest of us will just have to stand in for him." His blue eyes held compassion while his deep voice relayed his conviction. "We're all praying for Danny. He's a fighter."

"He sure is."

"And so are you, Granger."

Tears stung her eyes, and she fought to keep them at bay. She gave him a nod of thanks and reached for a change of subject. She sniffed once and swiped at her right eye where one tear had managed its escape.

"How's Megan doing? Does she enjoy being home with Alexander?"

Their little boy was fixing to be a year old in a couple of weeks. Megan worked for the hospital as a nurse, but once Alexander was born, she'd decided to leave her job to be a stay-at-home mom.

"She loves it. I like it, too. It's nice because, when I'm off work, we can do things together as a family. There's no trying to keep our schedules straight. I think she'll probably go back to work once Alexander's in school, but we've got a few years to figure that out."

"That's great. I can't believe he's going to be one already. It seems like he was just born, and you were bringing him in to meet us, yesterday." After testing the fans, Leslie stored them back on the truck and started to inventory the search and rescue equipment.

"Tell me about it. He took his first step yesterday." Bryce grinned, the pride evident in the way his eyes twinkled.

"Oh, my goodness! That's amazing. Okay, now there's no stopping him, and nothing is safe." She laughed. "Are they coming by for lunch today?"

"No, not today. Megan's mom wanted to take them shopping and find Alexander some clothes for his birthday."

Leslie couldn't wait to see Clint when he showed up for dinner tonight. She was glad he was coming and didn't regret inviting him, but she was already preparing herself for the teasing that was bound to happen.

She lowered her voice a little. "Hey, Clint Baker is coming by to eat with us tonight."

Bryce had just finished putting the last of the ventilation equipment back on board. He turned, one eyebrow raised in curiosity. "Is he coming in an official capacity or..."

"Yes?" It was good for a police presence to show up at the station off and on. But she really invited him because not seeing him for a full twenty-four hours sounded like torture.

Apparently, that was all the answer Bryce needed. He chuckled. "And you'd like me to run interference?"

Their friend and fellow firefighter, Chet Holden, never missed an opportunity to tease them. Especially if it had to do with something in their personal life. He was a great guy, and normally she took it in stride, but she didn't want him to make Clint feel uncomfortable.

It wasn't all that long ago that Bryce invited Megan to

join them for her first meal at the station. Now she was just another member of their large family.

"I'll do my best. But you know what it's like around here..."

"Yep." And she wouldn't trade it for anything.

It was maddening the way Christopher King kept his hands clasped on top of the table in front of him and answered each question Detective Paris threw at him without missing a beat. Every answer was immediate, to the point, with nothing added that wasn't requested. The guy had missed his calling as an undercover agent for the CIA.

Clint was in the room with them, his ankle crossed over his left knee, doing his best to look interested but not in a hurry. They needed King to know that they expected answers, but their case didn't revolve around him.

"I'm going to ask you again, why was there a scanner in the janitorial closet, and why were the only fingerprints on it yours?" Paris sat in a chair opposite the table from King and leveled him with a look that would've made most suspects uneasy.

King stared right back. "And like I already told you, I found it sitting in the hallway. I didn't want someone to trip over it, so I put it in the closet to get it out of the way. I had no way of knowing whether it had any fingerprints on it." His gaze was steady. Unnaturally so.

"Had you ever seen anyone else use a scanner like that in the building?"

"No."

Clint leaned forward slightly. "Why were you at the back of the warehouse so near the fire? You should have evacuated the building when the alarm sounded like everyone else."

King's gaze flicked to him with the same level of non-emotion. "I wanted to make sure everyone else had gotten out. It's my job to keep the employees safe, with or without a fire."

Before bringing him in for questioning, Clint had reached out to Chief Menendez at fire station two and asked about King's condition when the firefighters had located him. They said he seemed confused and panicked. A far cry from how he was acting now. Either the guy crumbled under real emergencies like the fire, or he was a good actor. Was he acting *now*, or was his real performance back in the warehouse?

They knew he wasn't the actual shooter. Keyes and Cho had gotten him out of the warehouse before Danny had become a target. But the further they got into this investigation, the more Clint was convinced the shooter—whoever he was—hadn't been acting alone.

Paris must've been thinking along the same lines. "Did you get turned around in the warehouse?"

"Yes, between the smoke and the electricity being turned off, it was easy to get confused."

"Did you see anyone else while you were clearing the building?"

"No one. It seemed everyone else had gotten out already. Which is a good thing." For the first time since he'd come in for questioning, the corners of King's mouth lifted up in a smile that didn't quite reach his eyes. "I'm thankful none of my co-workers were hurt in the fire."

"As are we, I assure you." Paris stood. "Unfortunately, there's still a firefighter that's fighting for his life right now. A man who was originally in there looking for you."

Again, no physical or obvious emotional reaction.

"I hope he makes a full recovery."

Clint doubted the guy cared one bit about Danny or anyone else. He suspected that, if King had really been in danger from the fire inside of the warehouse, he would've been one of the first to leave regardless of whether his co-workers had gotten out yet or not.

Paris stood, and Clint followed suit.

"Thank you for coming in. You are free to go. I'll have Officer Carrington give you a ride back home. We'll be in touch if we have any more questions."

King stood and nodded. "Whatever I can do to help."

Clint followed Paris out of the room and back to the conference room where he closed the door behind them.

Paris sat on the edge of the table. "What's your take?"

"I don't believe a word he says." Clint jabbed his hands into his pants pockets. "It all sounded rehearsed. Like he was repeating something he'd read or thought through a million times, with no emotion behind it."

"I agree. We know he wasn't the shooter, but I'm willing to bet he knows who is. Whether King's covering for someone else or just trying to keep from getting caught himself, it's hard to know. I'm going to have someone sit on him and watch his place. Let's see if anyone tries to get in touch with him. In the meantime, check in with Logan. See if those financials have come in yet."

"I'm on it."

Clint walked through the bullpen and down the hall to where Logan's office was. The man's desk was a technological marvel with multiple landscape monitors mounted on the wall above it. There was something different pulled up on each one.

Logan sat in a black and red desk chair that looked more like something a gamer would use.

The moment Clint entered through the open door, Logan looked up.

"You're here about..."

"Christopher King's financials."

"Ah!" He pulled a file up on the third monitor. Clearly the man had multiple things going on at the same time.

Clint admired his ability to keep track of them all like he did.

"Here we go." Logan pointed to a set of bank statements. "According to these, King gets a paycheck weekly. That paycheck has been pretty consistent through the two years he's worked for the paper company. It looks like he earned a small raise last Christmas, which is reflected here." He used his mouse to highlight the first time the pay amount had increased. "Now, here's where it gets interesting. Starting about five months ago, he began to deposit five hundred dollars into his checking account every Monday."

"That's pretty unusual. Any idea where he's getting the money from?"

"None. He deposits cash, he does it himself, and he always uses the drive through at the bank. Five hundred dollars at a time like that isn't a large enough sum to cause the bank any concern. I checked the bank's security." Logan's hands flew over the keyboard until a picture of King, seated in the front seat of his car, popped up on the monitor. "And it's always him, and he's always alone in the car."

"Has there been an increase in his spending?"

"No, he's just been adding to the balance in his account. There's nothing else unusual going on, at least not on paper."

"Could you send a picture of King to my phone please?"

"You've got it."

"All right, Logan, thanks."

Clint pulled his phone out as he left the office. He wanted to send Leslie a picture of King and give her an update. It'd be good if she at least knew what he looked like in case he showed up at the station.

Chapter Twenty-Three

L eslie was on the phone with Becca when she got a text from Clint immediately followed by a phone call that she couldn't answer before it went to voicemail. As soon as she hung up with Becca, she checked the text to find a photo of a man but no explanation. She called Clint back.

He answered on the first ring. "Hey, I was leaving you a voice message, but this is better."

"Sorry I missed your call. I was on the phone with Becca." She'd gone to the kitchen area while talking, and several of her co-workers were nearby and clearly listening in. No doubt they were anxious for word about Danny, and she couldn't blame them. She raised her voice slightly to make sure they could hear what she was about to tell Clint. "Becca says his fever broke early this morning. The doctor is continuing the IV antibiotics to be safe, but he's hopeful that quick response to the infection means Danny will be in the clear soon."

Her fellow firefighters all grinned with relief and nodded their approval.

"That's great, Leslie. I'm so relieved to hear that. Do they have any idea how much longer he'll be in the hospital?"

"Nothing definitive. The doctor mentioned the possibility of going home on Saturday but that they'll know more tomorrow."

"Still, that's wonderful news."

"So, I got this picture you texted me. What's going on?"

Clint told her about the interview with Christopher King.

"He isn't the shooter, but there's more to this guy than he lets on, and Paris and I are confident he's involved in some way. He strikes me as the type who'll keep his nose clean to keep from drawing more attention to himself, but I wanted to make sure you have his picture. Show it around the station. If anyone sees this man, please let me know immediately."

Anger flared in her chest. If this guy was involved at all, then he put all of their lives in danger—and especially Bryce and Jin who were the ones who found King and got him out of the warehouse. The very idea that King might have been playing them all was unacceptable.

"You okay?" Clint must have sensed her fury in the silence between them. "I promise you, honey, we will get these guys." He emphasized every word of his last sentence.

His determination combined with the first time he'd used a term of endearment, and Leslie's heart swelled with gratitude that not only was Clint on her side, but that he was becoming such a big part of her life.

"I know. Thank you."

"I have to run. Be careful. I'll touch base again later."

"Yeah, you be careful, too."

The information she had about King weighed heavy as she ended the call.

Bryce and Chet, who were still in the room, immediately approached. Bryce put a supportive hand on her shoulder. "What is it?"

"An update from Clint. I need to speak to the chief. Then it's something everyone needs to see."

Ten minutes later, Menendez had everyone gather in the meeting room. Leslie had sent the picture of King to his phone, and he had it up on the large smart board.

"Some of you may recognize this man. His name is Christopher King. When we responded to the fire at the warehouse, he was the security guard that was unaccounted for. Keyes and Cho, you located him and were able to get him out of the warehouse safely. However, it has now come to the attention of the DPD that King may have had a hand in setting the fire and informing the suspect who shot Bracken when we got to the building."

Angry murmurs filled the room as everyone spoke of their disbelief.

Jin stood from his chair. "You're telling me that idiot may have had us in there looking for him for no reason? Did he start the fire?"

"Is he in police custody?"

"Do we know who actually shot Danny?"

Menendez raised his hand to try and quiet the group. "First of all, we have to remember that these are just allegations at this point. The DPD is still working on getting solid evidence. Until then, they didn't have enough to charge him, and they're hoping he'll lead them to the shooter or they'll be able to find irrefutable proof that he was involved." He walked over and tapped the TV screen. "If he knew what was good for him, guilty or not, he'd stay holed up in his house somewhere out of sight. But if you see him, whether here at the station or at any call out locations, we need to know about it immediately."

The chief took a moment to meet each of their eyes before speaking again. "It's imperative that this information stays within the department. Is that understood?"

Everyone acknowledged his orders. Bryce was just about to ask a question when the station alarm sounded.

They were the closest station to a residential fire. A shop behind the house was involved, and there was concern that the fire could jump to the house or even possibly the neighbor's house.

Their engine company was activated, and within minutes, they were driving out of the station, their lights flashing and siren blaring.

As she always did, Leslie said a prayer that her fellow firefighters would stay safe.

Menendez went back to his office to take a phone call. That left Leslie, Bryce, Chet, and Jin to wander to the kitchen. She wasn't sure any of them were hungry, but the weight of knowing about King was a lot to deal with.

Chet pulled a plate of chocolate chip cookies from the fridge and set them on the counter. Leslie grabbed one and took a bite, but even the chocolate barely registered as it hit her tongue.

Jin flopped into a chair with a growl. "I hate that this makes me second guess everything." He addressed Leslie. "I mean, did the guy go way into the back of the warehouse just to draw us away from you and Danny? Was it the luck of the draw—and if we'd swapped search areas, would it have been me and Keyes that were targeted?"

"I don't know." Thinking about the possibilities gave

Leslie a headache. "I wish we knew something definitively. None of this makes sense."

Jin glowered as he ate a cookie in two bites and reached for another.

The station alarm sounded again, and this time the alert came up on Leslie's phone along with the rest of the ladder company.

Cookies abandoned, they put on their gear and made their way to the ladder truck for a call out to a structure fire on the edge of town not far from the station. A large barn was on fire, and it was filled with hay and feed.

Leslie knew from experience that the entire thing was going to go up in minutes because of how flammable the contents of the barn were. But they needed to get the fire put out before it spread to any fields or structures nearby.

Minutes later, they were on their way with Bryce behind the wheel.

Leslie stared at Danny's empty spot, and her heart ached. She had to remind herself that he was going to be okay. Soon, they'd be working together again, and the people who put him in the hospital would be behind bars.

"Granger." Chet's voice came over communications.

Her gaze snapped away from Danny's seat to find Chet watching her in the rearview mirror from the passenger seat up front. As the ladder company officer, he was the one who kept them running efficiently.

"I need your head in the game. Are you good?"

He was right. She needed to focus so she could do her job and not be a liability for her company.

"I'm good, Lieutenant."

With a single nod, he turned his attention back on the road in front of them.

The fire was located on a family farm that was down several small roads once they got off the highway. As they approached the farm, the owners had already opened the large double gate and were waving them in. As soon as the truck made it through, the couple got onto their ATV and followed.

The smoke wasn't visible until they followed the driveway around the house to the back of the property. A red barn came into view. It was relatively small with double doors that rolled open like a garage door and another normal-sized door beside that. Across the rest of the front were windows, and it looked like there were some down the sides as well.

To Leslie's surprise, the barn itself wasn't engulfed at all. In fact, the only thing she could see burning was a stack of hay bales sitting out front. Flames were quickly consuming the dry hay and beginning to lick the side of the barn, blistering the dark red paint.

They all immediately got out of the ladder truck and got to work as Chet called out assignments.

"Cho, grab the water can and see if you can get that under control. Keyes, let's get this line stretched and ready in case we need it. Granger, find the breaker box and kill the electricity."

Leslie noted where the electrical pole was and the line coming off it going behind the barn. She jogged past the barn and around back to find the breaker box attached to the rear of the building. Hastily, she opened it and flipped the main breaker, cutting off electricity to the barn and making it safer for them to enter the building if they needed to.

When she got back to the ladder truck, Jin was using the pressurized water extinguisher to douse the flames traveling up the side of the barn. Bryce had gotten the line hooked up and was holding the nozzle.

"Cho," Chet called across the way. "Fall back. You and Granger back up the line."

Cho stopped using the extinguisher and set it down next to the truck before picking up the hose, and Leslie took up her place behind him.

Bryce opened the nozzle, and water began to flow. Leslie worked with Jin to absorb the force created by the water and provide stability so that Bryce could maintain control as he directed a stream of water onto the hay bales as well as the side of the barn.

It took next to no time to put the fire out, leaving a steaming stack of blackened hay. There was certainly some aesthetic damage to the outside of the barn, but it didn't look like there would be any structural damage.

They all removed their helmets and set them on the truck.

Leslie had noticed that the couple who lived on the farm had been watching them from their ATV and were now on foot and approaching.

"Thank you. Thank you so much." The man reached out to shake Chet's hand. "I'm Gary Tippin, and this is my wife, Francie. We appreciate your quick response."

"Of course. I'm glad the fire wasn't any worse. You'll want to take a look and make sure there's no damage to the wood along that wall, but I suspect most of the damage is cosmetic. This type of fire can spread quickly. Honestly, I'm surprised that it wasn't worse. You must've seen the fire the moment it broke out."

The couple looked at each other in confusion, and Francie shook her head. "Our dog started barking like crazy, so Gary went to look out the back window to see what he was barking at. That's when he saw some smoke coming out of the hay bales and then flames. I immediately called 9-1-1, but they said that someone had already reported the fire, and that a unit was on the way. I'd barely had the chance to tell Gary when we heard the sirens. We had to rush to get the gate open for you all."

Someone else had called it in? Leslie hadn't even noticed the smoke until they had neared the Tippin's house. She took in the area around them. The house and barn stood in a large clearing that included at least an acre between them. But beyond that, trees and shrubs lined the property. There was no way someone had seen the smoke from the road or a neighboring house.

Goosebumps peppered her skin, and the hair stood on the back of her neck. She had the unmistakable feeling they were being watched... followed by an urgency she couldn't explain.

Chapter Twenty-Four

Leslie sidled up to Chet. She lowered her voice. "Something's not right. I think we need to get out of the open and call in the police."

"Agreed." Chet didn't hesitate. He turned to the older couple. "Mr. and Mrs. Tippin, why don't we go inside and take a look around. Make sure none of that fire damage came through the wall." He gave Leslie a nod as he quickly escorted the couple into the barn.

Mr. Tippin had to dig his keys out to unlock the regular door. As he did, the urgency she'd been feeling intensified.

Come on, come on, come on!

Mr. Tippin got the door open. Leslie ignored the urge to look over her shoulder as she spoke to Jin and Bryce. "Guys, we need to get inside. I think the shooter set the fire and he's still out—"

A gunshot pierced the air.

Wooden splinters flew as a bullet struck the side of the barn near the door.

All three firefighters ducked and ran for the doorway.

Another gunshot, and a burning pain erupted in Leslie's upper arm.

They worked together to close the barn door to provide more coverage from the gunfire. Light filtered in through the large glass windows making it possible for them to see inside, but it also meant the shooter could potentially see them as well.

Chet was helping the Tippins get onto the ground and under a workbench along one wall. As soon as they were set, he spoke into his radio linking them to dispatch. "We have gunshots fired at our location. We and the residents are inside the barn behind the house."

Jin, Bryce, and Leslie dropped to their hands and knees, a motion made difficult by their turnout gear. Her co-workers began to shed their boots, pants, and jackets. While their gear was absolutely essential when fighting fires, the weight and thickness made it difficult to move around freely, to take cover, or, God forbid, fight the gunman if he forced his way into the barn.

Fear swept through Leslie. Dispatch would make sure they got help, but she needed to call Clint and tell him this was the same shooter from the warehouse.

Sweat beaded on her forehead and dripped down her back as the phone barely rang once before he picked it up.

"Leslie? A call just came in—"

"That's us. He called in the fire before it was even set."

A gun shot shattered another window sending glass everywhere. Mrs. Tippin yelped.

"He's got us cornered in the barn."

"We're on our way. Stay where you're at."

She nodded, even though there was no way he could see it. She tried to form words for a response, but her brain wouldn't cooperate. Why was she so hot?

Bryce must have noticed her discomfort because his eyes narrowed as he positioned himself in front of her. "Leslie? Hey, let's get that jacket off you." He started to help her with it when his eyes widened. "You've been hit."

Hit? She stared at him and tried to figure out what he meant.

"Leslie?" Clint's voice came from the phone.

Bryce took it from her. "This is Keyes. We're going to need an ambulance. Leslie's been hit." Another gunshot pierced the air. "I'm gonna have to set the phone down and see how bad this is. Be careful when you arrive, the shooter's still out there. I think the shots were coming from the west or northwest, but I'm not sure."

Leslie worked to even her breathing as Bryce and Jin helped her get her jacket off as well as the pants and boots, leaving her in cotton leggings, a T-shirt, and socks.

The cool air breezed over her damp skin, bringing relief and a little clarity to her mind. She winced when Bryce applied a handkerchief to her left upper arm. "How bad is it?"

"Looks like the bullet just grazed you, but it's bleeding pretty good." Bryce studied her face. "You with us?"

"Yeah, I'm better now." It bothered her that the combination of being overheated, the stress, and the wound had muddled her brain so much for a few moments there.

Bryce snatched the phone off the ground and gave an update to Clint.

The silence from outside the barn was nearly as deafening as the gunshots. Had he run off? Or was he approaching the barn?

Chet and the Tippins were already out of sight of the windows. Jin, Bryce, and Leslie scooted closer to the wall and ducked into the small space under another workbench.

Jin looked around and reached for a large axe that was leaning against the wall. He shoved it across the barn floor to Chet.

"There's a shotgun in the cabinet over there," Mr. Tippin pointed.

Bryce motioned for Jin to take over putting pressure on Leslie's wound and crawled over to the cabinet. As soon as he had the shotgun in his hands, he made sure it was loaded and came back, positioning himself low to the ground between them and the door.

Leslie noted a shovel nearby. If push came to shove, she'd wield that to keep their attacker at bay. They may not be trained for this, but none of them were going to face the shooter without a fight.

The air was unnaturally quiet as Clint gripped his handgun and followed Paris. No doubt the shooting earlier had scared off much of the wildlife. They'd parked in front of the house and were making their way around toward the barn. Two other officers were circling around to the left while another pair were doing the same to the right—all searching for someone hiding in the trees around the edge of the property.

Clint kept his eyes on the tree line as they made their way past the house and to the ladder truck, which they would use as a shield if the situation changed.

It was frustrating to know that Leslie was in the barn just a few hundred feet away, and he couldn't get to her yet. All he wanted was to clear the area and get in there. See for himself that Leslie was okay.

Paris spoke into his two-way radio. "How are we looking? Is there any movement in the trees?"

"Negative. Nothing on the east side. Continuing to work our way around."

"Carrington here on the west. We've got flattened grass and weeds with numerous shell casings. There's a direct view of the barn from here. No visual on the shooter."

"Understood. We're moving in now."

Together, Clint and Paris rounded the fire truck and quickly made their way across the open space to the barn. The hose the firefighters had been using to put out the fire still lay stretched across the dry grass. The scent of burned hay and smoke lingered in the air.

When they reached the door, Paris gave Clint a nod.

"This is Officer Baker. Detective Paris is here, too. It looks like we're in the clear, although other officers are in the process of verifying that. We're coming in."

Scuffling noises from the other side were followed by the door opening.

Keyes was standing just inside, a shotgun in hand. He stepped back so they could enter. "It's been quiet out there for at least six or seven minutes, but we didn't know if that meant he'd left or if he was coming in closer. With all the windows... Well, it's not a great place to be stuck but a whole lot better than being out in the open.

Holden was helping an older couple get to their feet. "We never even saw him, but it was clear the fire had been set to lure us here."

Leslie was still sitting on the ground. Cho was beside her, pressing a cloth against her upper arm. Blood had dribbled all the way down to her fingers.

Clint strode forward and lowered to one knee beside

her. He placed a hand against her upper back, thankful to feel her breathing and have that physical proof she was alive. "How are we looking?"

"The bullet grazed her, but she's definitely going to need some stitches." Cho pulled the cloth back to reveal a nasty gash that oozed blood the moment there wasn't any pressure.

"Here, I'll take that." Clint switched positions with Cho and took over keeping the cloth pressed against her wound and continued to keep one on her back. He raised his head and looked around. "Was anyone else injured?"

Except for a few small cuts from falling glass, everyone else seemed to be fine. Paris called out to have the ambulance, which was waiting on the road just off the property, come on in.

Leslie rested her head on his shoulder. "I'm so glad you're here."

"And I'm glad you're okay. You scared me, Granger." He let his forehead fall to rest against her temple. "Can you stand?"

"For the record, it wasn't too fun in here, either." She let him help her to her feet. "Yeah. I think I'm okay now."

Confused, Clint looked to Keyes for an explanation.

"We thought she was going to pass out earlier between being overheated in the gear and losing blood."

"I wasn't about to pass out," she objected.

But the look Keyes gave him over her head said differently.

Clint put an arm around her for extra support. The cloth he held against her arm was sticky with blood.

Carrington's voice came through the radio. "The area is clear, and the ambulance is approaching now. You're good to exit the barn."

"Come on. Let's get you to the hospital."

Paris opened the door, and Clint led the way with Leslie. He was going to tell Paris that he planned to ride in the ambulance with her, but he didn't need to. His friend simply clapped him on the shoulder and said, "I'll keep you updated."

Cho, Keyes, and Holden promised they'd check on her soon and take care of her gear in the meantime.

Within minutes, they got settled into the back of the ambulance. An EMT he knew, Rory, pressed a stack of clean gauze to Leslie's arm and gave her a comforting smile. "Once we get to the hospital, they'll have you stitched up in no time."

Clint sat on the bench nearby and held her hand in his. Her skin was chilled. She shivered, and Rory pulled a blanket out of one of the storage compartments and spread it out over her patient.

He knew the shaking was likely due to the adrenaline fading, but he was also worried about blood loss. He'd feel better once the doctor examined her.

"Hey." Leslie's soft voice drew his attention to her face. "I'm okay."

"Yeah. It was the not knowing for a while there... Just promise me you won't put me through anything like that again." He was making light of it, but seriously, she'd been hurt, and he had no idea how bad the injury was. It had been one of the worst ten minutes of his life.

"I can promise that I'll never do it on purpose. Besides, now I can take 'getting shot' off my bucket list. So there's that." She smiled then, her eyes glittering with humor.

"That's not even funny." He leaned forward and brushed his lips against hers. "Seriously, you and I need to sit down and go over your bucket list."

He rested his hand on her forehead and lightly brushed his thumb over her hair. The shooter could have easily killed Lesley today.

Things between them were still so new, but more and more, he found himself picture a future together.

Chapter Twenty-Five

Bree put her chubby little arm across Leslie's chest and snuggled in close. Leslie breathed in the scent of her niece's strawberry-scented shampoo.

"Thank you, sweetie." She kissed the top of her head.

Leslie wasn't sure what was going to be reported on the news, so she'd texted Cindy to let her know what happened and reassure her that she was okay. She never expected her sister to bring the girls to check on her. It was sweet, and the girls were certainly helping to distract Leslie from the wait for her discharge papers to go through.

"Auntie? Does it hurt?" Izzy stared at the white bandage, concern filling her eyes. "It looks like it hurts."

"Yeah, it does. A little." It'd taken seven stitches to close up the wound. Even with extra strength acetaminophen in her system, she could still feel the throb when she was perfectly still, much less if she moved her arm around. "But it'll heal fast and be good as new."

Leslie was pretty sure it was going to leave quite a scar. It was a small price to pay for her life, and she'd thanked God for His mercies ever since Clint had entered that barn.

Speaking of Clint, he'd stepped out of the room when Cindy and the kids had come by. She imagined he was probably waiting in the hallway to give them space. Was it silly she already missed him?

"Are you sure you don't want to stay at my house for a while?"

It was sweet of Cindy to offer, but Leslie had politely declined.

"I'll be fine. I don't think there's a whole lot I can't do on my own. Besides, I have a feeling sleeping may be the hardest part. If I'm up and down a lot through the night, I don't want to worry about waking you all."

The gunman was still out there, and that was Leslie's greatest concern. The last thing she wanted to do was involve her sister and the kids by staying at their house. She didn't say that now, though, because she didn't want to scare the girls. A more detailed conversation with Cindy was in order once Leslie got discharged and could give her a call.

The sweet, cuddly moments with Bree were over as the little one climbed off the hospital bed and tried to open the cabinet doors by the sink. Cindy swept her up and got a squeal of protest.

"Mom? I'm hungry." Izzy put a hand on her stomach and patted it dramatically. "My tummy wants Chick-Fil-A."

Leslie looked at the clock. It was well after six. So much for having dinner with Clint and the crew at the fire station.

Cindy's chuckle ended in a groan as Bree tried to squirm out of her arms. "It looks like our time here has ended. Will you please call me when you get home?"

"I will. Thank you for stopping by. It means a lot." She used two fingers and pointed them at her eyes and then at Izzy. "You behave yourself, little lady."

Izzy copied the movements. "I will!" She turned her

attention to her mom. "I'll bet your tummy would like Chick-Fil-A, too."

"How am I supposed to argue with that? Come on, girls, let's let Auntie get some rest."

Bree waved as the three of them left.

The door had barely closed before it opened again, and Clint slipped inside.

"The nurse just told me she'll be by with your discharge papers in a minute." He came around to stand by the bed. "It was nice of Bryce to bring your duffel bag from the station."

She'd changed from her sweat-soaked leggings into a pair of jeans. She could do that by herself, but she did have to have a little help from the nurse to change into a fresh shirt. A minor issue to deal with once she got back home. She'd figure it out, though.

"Have you heard anything from Detective Paris? Did they find anything helpful at the scene? Are the Tippins okay?"

With so much going on, she really hated being stuck in the hospital.

"I don't know anything yet, but Paris said they're meeting at one to go over everything. He was hoping you could look through some old call outs and see if anything jogs your memory, but he can bring the files by your place if you're not up to going to the precinct."

Finally, she'd have something to focus on. She hopped off the table and ignored the way the jostle sent a stab of pain through her arm. "I'm ready, willing, and able."

"Whoa, there." Clint slipped an arm around her waist and gently tugged her close. "Between doctors, nurses, and your sister, it's been like a train station in here. I need a minute to hold you."

One of his hands cupped the back of her head as he folded her into his arms in a hug that she desperately needed.

"I didn't like not being there to protect you," he murmured near her ear.

"I know. I realized today that it would be hard for both of us. Every time I hear a siren, I'll wonder if it's you and if you're safe. And I imagine you'll feel the same when you see a fire truck driving down the street or hear about a fire." She realized she'd spoken as though they were together and were talking about their future as a couple. They'd never even come close to having that conversation.

Her cheeks heated, and she pressed her forehead against his chest. "I'm sorry. The last few days have been intense. I don't even know if you want... if we'll still see each other when all of this is over."

Clint stepped back and cradled her face with hands. He waited for her to look up and meet his eyes. "I very much want to keep seeing you when all of this is over. I know there's a lot to deal with when it comes to our schedules and some of the dangers of our professions, but we can handle them as they come. Honey, I'm all in if you are."

Her heart stuttered in her chest at the intensity and emotion in his eyes. He hadn't said he loved her, but she could see the truth of it in his eyes. There would be time for those declarations.

For now, she knew that she wanted to see where this went, too. "Yeah. I'm all in."

With a look that reflected the wonder in her own heart, he leaned in and kissed her gently, slowly, and with a promise that this was only the beginning of something amazing.

"Ahem."

Leslie wasn't sure which of them broke the kiss, but when she opened her eyes, she saw the nurse standing there looking amused.

"I've got your discharge papers ready. Assuming you still want them."

"Definitely." She reached for them with her uninjured arm. "Thank you."

The nurse had already gone over the after care, and it would be relatively simple to follow. Lifting her arm would be a challenge, and it meant she'd be wearing a lot of button-down shirts for a week or two.

Still, she'd take it. At this point, she'd give anything to catch the person responsible so that her biggest worry was how she was going to get dressed in the morning.

Chapter Twenty-Six

Clint looked over at Leslie seated next to him at the conference room table and sent up a silent prayer of thanks that things today hadn't turned out differently. She was here, she was healthy, and she was safe.

Even after all she'd been through, Leslie looked like she was ready to tackle anything that was thrown her way.

Right now, she was busy studying the large whiteboard at the front of the room. There was an extensive amount of information, and even though he'd shared a lot about the investigation, he hadn't told her everything.

Along with Detective Paris, Carrington, Smith, and Logan also joined them for the meeting.

Paris stood and addressed Leslie. "Miss Granger, I think I speak for everyone here when I say I'm glad that you're okay, and that you've come in to assist us."

Murmurs of agreement filled the room.

"Please, just call me Leslie."

Paris gave her a friendly smile. "At this point, we must assume that the suspect has some kind of personal connection to you. We need to find out what that is. Once we do, then we can identify him and get him into custody before he hurts anyone else."

"I'm happy to help in any way I can."

Paris nodded his appreciation. "There's nothing about this guy that seems familiar to you?"

"Nothing. I've been wracking my brain trying to figure out a connection. I mean, someone this angry has to have a reason. At least something he sees as a reason, anyway. It makes no sense. Wouldn't he *want* me to know why he's targeting me?"

"One would think so," Clint agreed. "Nothing about this is random. It seems like our two main possibilities are stalking and revenge."

Paris wrote them on the white board. "But again, a stalker wants attention and usually tries to get positive attention before it turns abusive or deadly. As for an individual bent on revenge, Leslie's right. He'd want you to know why he's doing this to you."

"Maybe there's some kind of indirect attention," Carrington suggested. "A situation where the suspect blames Leslie but doesn't have a direct contact to her. He doesn't care if she knows why he's trying to hurt her as long as he completes his mission. If there was a personal connection, why not simply shoot her? Why shoot Danny Bracken and then go through all this to scare her?" He cringed and turned to Leslie. "Sorry."

She held up a hand to stop him. "No apologies necessary. They're legitimate questions."

The thought of everything that Leslie had been through over the last few days made Clint's blood boil. Especially when he thought about how right Carrington was. "He was probably watching the whole time the fire department was working that fire earlier. He could have shot Leslie at any time. He waited until they ran into the barn. I'm not sure he intended to kill her so much as hurt or scare her."

Paris lifted a stack of files and placed them in front of Leslie. "I know this is a lot, but these are the calls that your station has received in the last year that either ended up being arson or where someone was seriously injured or killed. I weeded out the calls that you weren't working on. If you could look through these, you might see something that seems to click with what's going on."

"Of course." She immediately opened the first file and began to read through it.

"Logan, have you been able to make any connection between Christopher King and Domingo Ortiz?"

"Originally? No." Logan pointed to the large television where he'd shared his laptop's screen. A picture of each man was visible. "However, I may actually have something." He made the picture of King bigger. "We know that King works as a security guard at the warehouse. I decided to dig deeper and found out that he works for an employment agency that specializes in security. The paper company pays the agency, and then the agency hires and pays King. A lot of people who go through employment agencies will work at more than one place." With a flare, he pulled up a picture of a brick building. "It turns out, he also works at a local out-patient rehabilitation center, New Beginnings, that treats a variety of emotional and psychological illnesses."

"Let me guess," Paris interjected. "That's the center where Ortiz is receiving his therapy services."

Logan pointed at him with a triumphant smile. "We've got a winner. Now, I have no way of knowing whether the two of them ever interacted."

Clint had a hard time believing it was a coincidence.

"Maybe they both have a connection to the shooter. Part of Ortiz's rehabilitation may be some group therapy session. Ortiz said his roommate, Rick Castor, was using his klepto-mania to blackmail him. We assumed he found out because Ortiz was bringing stuff back from the fire station, but what if Castor knew this before he decided to rent the apartment?"

"He was targeted." Paris nodded thoughtfully. "It's a good theory. We know King is getting money every week from someone. Maybe it's some kind of payment or kick-back originating at the rehabilitation center, and Castor found out about it. Once he did, he could've forced King to let him into the warehouse and tell him when the fire department had arrived on scene. If King was into anything illegal, he would've done anything Castor wanted or risk losing his job and ever working in the secu-rity field again." He looked at Carrington. "You and Smith go pick up King and bring him back for more ques-tioning."

King was brought in, and he still held onto his emotionless exterior until Paris produced the bank records showing the five hundred dollars he was receiving every Monday. Only then did King's face pale.

Clint knew they were onto something.

"We have a blackmail victim that's connected to New Beginnings. Another business that you happen to work for as a security guard." Paris paused. "Who's been giving you the money?"

"It's a gift from a family member." King's gaze flicked down and to the left.

"If that's the case, a quick call to that family member to verify is all we need, and you'll be on your way."

King sat, his spine rod-straight, and looked Paris right in the eyes. "I'm not saying anything else until I speak with a lawyer."

Disappointment hit Clint like a physical blow. They could do nothing else until a lawyer was located and brought in for King. It'd take some time—time they couldn't afford to waste.

Paris had King taken into holding for the next seventy-two hours, and Clint returned to the conference room to check on Leslie.

It'd been nearly two hours since she started looking through the files, and she was clearly spent. She held her arm close to her body. Her eyes, dimmed by exhaustion and pain, met his.

She'd created two piles for the folders: one for those that she didn't think had any connection whatsoever. And another for those she thought might be a possibility. "I'm only putting them in that pile because either I remember how upset the person was, because I personally spoke to them, or both."

Logan was going through the second stack and using his computer to check on the individuals involved.

Clint rested a hand on her shoulder. "Hey, we should get you home. You need to get some rest before you fall over."

She shook her head, her hair moving back and forth over his hand. "I've only got three left. I'll finish these, and then we can go."

Now, Clint was feeling useless. He wished he could go through the files with her at least. He glanced across the table at Logan. "Is there anyone that stands out yet?"

"I haven't finished looking at the ones she pulled out. But so far, I'm not finding any connection between them."

Leslie used her good arm to gather her hair and pull it over her shoulder. "Hold on a second, I may have something. I remember this fire." She tapped the folder.

"I'm going to get Paris back in here." Clint found the detective in his office, and they both returned within minutes.

Once they were seated, Paris motioned for Leslie to continue.

"It was a four-story apartment building. Several stations responded to the call because, by the time we got there, a section of the third floor was fully involved. My company was responsible for going in and helping people evacuate. It was horrible. There were several rescues from windows because the fire spread so fast that people on the fourth floor couldn't get down."

She stared at the table, her brows furrowed. "There was one man in particular who was really upset. He kept saying his wife was on the third floor and that we needed to rescue her. He told us which apartment it was. Unfortunately, that was an apartment near where the fire originated. It'd been completely engulfed for a while, and we couldn't even get to that section of the building. He grabbed my arm and begged me to go save her. Someone told him that it was too late and that there was nothing left of that part of the building. He tried to push past us to go in and get her himself." She shook her head, her eyes heavy with sorrow. "Danny and I stopped him from going in, and someone from the police department pulled him away from the building."

"That's horrible." Logan frowned. "I can't even imagine going through that. From any angle. I think I remember that fire. It wasn't all that long ago." He started typing on his laptop.

Clint wanted desperately to help ease the pain the memory was clearly eliciting.

Paris cleared his throat. "I take it his wife did die in the fire?"

"There's no way she made it. There were two fatalities that day." She looked at the file again. "The names of the victims are in there—both women. But I don't see the names of the surviving family members."

"I've got it," Logan announced. "One second... Yep. Okay, the fire took place... Whoa. It was one year ago last Monday." He raised his gaze from his laptop screen.

"What about the survivors of the two women who died?" Paris leaned forward, his forearms on the table.

"Bella Adams was in the apartment where the fire originated. She was survived by her son, Daniel, and her daughter, Karen. Her husband had passed five years prior. Let me see. The other victim was Marissa Boulder. She was survived by her husband—" Logan looked up sharply. "Jacob Boulder."

Clint sat up straighter. "Ortiz said that someone had referred to his roommate as Jake once."

Paris nodded. "What is the last known address for Jacob Boulder?"

Logan worked on his computer for several minutes and then sat back, his shoulders dropping. "I'm not seeing a current physical address for him, but he does rent a post office box on the other side of town."

"All right." Paris slapped his hands on the top of the table and stood. "It's late, and I'm sure the post office is closed. I'm going to try and contact someone, though. Logan, see if you can find a connection between Jacob Boulder, Ortiz, and King. Clint, take Leslie home. There's a good chance not much is going to happen overnight unless we get lucky. You may as well get some sleep."

Leslie must've been exhausted because she didn't even argue when he placed a hand against her back to escort her out of the conference room.

Some of the tension in his neck eased with the idea that they may be close. He had a strong suspicion that Jacob Boulder was their guy. Now they just had to track him down and bring him into custody.

Chapter Twenty-Seven

The sound of her cell phone ringing pierced Leslie's jumbled dream. She blinked as confusion and the remains of the dream muddled her mind. Where was she? She started to sit up, and her arm gave a painful twinge.

She was sleeping on the couch. That's right. It'd been Clint's suggestion. He thought it would help prevent her from accidentally rolling onto her injured arm in the middle of the night. Judging from the pain now, it was a good decision.

Her head dropped back onto the pillow, and she breathed in deep. It and the blanket smelled faintly of Clint's soap or deodorant. Whatever it was, it made her feel safe.

A text came through on her phone, reminding Leslie what woke her up in the first place.

More carefully this time, she sat up and reached for the phone as Clint padded out of the guest room in his bare feet.

"Are you okay?" He ran a hand through his tousled hair. "Do you need anything?"

"No, I'm okay. I missed a call—"

It was from Cindy, and it was almost one in the morning. The text was from her, too.

> Sorry to wake you, but I need your help.
> Bree's sick again, and I just dropped glass
> all over the kitchen floor.

Leslie tried to call her sister back, but it went to voicemail. Had Cindy cut herself on the glass? She pictured her sister trying to carry Bree while bleeding all over the floor. Maybe that's why she hadn't answered her call. She sent a text.

> Oh, no! Just leave the glass. I'll be there
> soon to help you clean it up.

She tossed her phone onto the coffee table, then told Curtis what was going on as she threw the blanket off her legs. "Cindy wouldn't have called this late if she didn't really need help. She might have cut herself on the glass. And trust me, when Bree isn't feeling well, she can be a screaming machine. I'm going to change quick."

"Let me know if you need any help. I'll get ready and drive you over."

The prospect of Clint helping her dress sent heat straight to her face. Suddenly she was aware of the fact that he was wearing a pair of sleep pants and a T-shirt that was tight enough to showcase all the muscles in his arms and chest. Between that and the messy hair...

Her throat dry, she forced herself to speak casually. "Yeah. Thank you." She hurried from the room.

Back at the hospital, she'd had the nurse help her into a clean bra and long-sleeved shirt, which she still wore. All she needed was a pair of jeans, which she managed to button with one hand. She slipped on her shoes and grabbed her purse.

Within minutes, they were in Clint's car on the way to Cindy's house. Not for the first time, Leslie was glad they lived on the same side of town.

As they pulled up to the house, Leslie noticed that most of the lights were on.

Clint helped her out of the car, and she was careful not to bump her arm on the door. She fished the keys from her pocket and started toward the house.

"Oh! Clint, could you grab my purse? I forgot it in the floorboard."

"Sure."

With a nod, she continued down the concrete path that led from the curb to the front door. She and Cindy had exchanged house keys just in case they ever needed them. She fished her keys out of her pocket.

The shrubs lined both sides of the small porch. The porch light wasn't on, so the only light illuminating the front came from the streetlight two houses down.

Leslie had just registered the smell of kerosene as she reached for the doorknob when someone grabbed her from behind and whipped her around to face the street. Her keys fell and skidded across the porch the porch and into the shrubs.

She barely had time to gasp before cold metal pressed against the side of her head.

"Stay quiet, or I'll pull the trigger right now." The voice, low and menacing, spoke next to her right ear.

"Put it down. Now."

Leslie's gaze swung to Clint, who was standing in the

middle of the pathway, his gun drawn. But her captor was holding her directly in front of him, so there was no way Clint could get a clean shot.

"If you take a step closer, I'll blow her head off." The man's voice dripped with disdain.

Panic flared, and she instinctively tried to move away from the gun. Her captor immediately grabbed her left arm and squeezed against the bullet wound from earlier. She let out a low groan of agony at the white-hot pain.

"You shoot her, and I promise you'll die." Clint's voice was calm. Even.

"I don't figure I'm walking away from this anyway, so I'm going to finish what I started." He pressed the muzzle of the gun even harder against her temple.

Leslie flinched. The idea that it could go off at any time sent shivers of fear down her spine. Her brain wanted to shut down with panic, but she needed to stay focused. Calm.

"My wife died because of you," the man snarled, his warm breath against her ear and neck.

"Jacob Boulder." The name rumbled from Clint's chest. "Marissa's death was not Leslie's fault."

His grip on her arm loosened in shock just a moment before tightening again. Leslie gasped, and her knees nearly went out from under her. She prayed Cindy was inside calling the police right now, and that she wouldn't try to open the door and put herself in Jacob's crosshairs.

"Don't even speak her name. You're not allowed to speak her name!" Jacob nearly shook with rage. "You have no idea what it's like to stand there and watch, knowing that the person you love more than anything is burning to death. And all because the people who are supposed to be heroes don't even try to save her."

"Please." Leslie flinched when he moved the muzzle of the gun forward just a little. "We couldn't go to those apartments on the third floor. They were already fully engulfed. The hallway in front of them was collapsing. I'm sorry, but your wife would've already passed before we even arrived on the scene."

It seemed so cold to say it like that, but it was the truth.

"I don't believe you. You took my wife from me, and now it's your turn to know exactly how it feels to lose someone you love to a fire."

Realization hit Leslie like a truck. It'd been Jacob who'd tried to call and text her, and it was all a ruse to get her here. But that meant he'd been inside the house and used Cindy's phone...

"What did you do to my sister and her kids?"

Rage dulled the pain in her arm and made her want to whirl around and try to fight back. But as long as he had that gun to her head, she'd be on the losing end of any battle.

"Oh, your nieces are still fast asleep in their little beds. But your sister? She didn't even know I was in the house. I tied her up and put her in the pantry. Trust me, I made sure she wasn't going to get out. She'll be trapped, just like my Marissa." He dropped her arm and reached into his pocket. He lifted a lighter up in front of her face, produced a flame with a click, and laughed.

Fresh fear surged as she realized he was going to set fire to her sister's house and then force her watch it burn with her family inside.

Seeing Leslie held at gunpoint filled Clint with a rage that he struggled to keep in check. He forced himself to breathe evenly and stay focused. He wished he had a way to call in for backup, but if he reached for his phone, then it would agitate Jacob further.

Leslie sagged a little when Jacob stopped squeezing her injured arm and pulled something out of his pocket. With a click, a flame appeared.

Clint tried to grasp what was happening. Jacob had broken into the house, tied up Leslie's sister, and he knew there were two little girls still in there. Yet, it was clear the deranged man was more than willing to set the whole place on fire and burn them alive.

The situation was deteriorating quickly. He needed to buy them some time and then pray that an opportunity would present itself.

"Jacob. Look at me." Clint's voice brought the other man's attention to him. "You haven't killed anyone yet. You can still come back from this."

"No." Jacob shook his head as he sneered. "I don't care. Drop your gun. Now."

If Clint put his gun down, he had no doubt Jacob would shoot him, then he would be no use to Leslie or Cindy and the kids. Right now, Jacob wanted to hurt Leslie more than he wanted to kill her. And while he might not care if he died once his point had been made, he certainly didn't want to be stopped now.

Clint's best option was to wait and pray for an opening to take the guy out. "I'm not going to do that."

Jacob growled as he clenched the lighter in his hand. The small flame cast an eerie orange glow on Leslie's face. She squeezed her eyes shut.

Please, God, give Leslie strength and keep her head clear. Calm Jacob. Help me to know what to do when it's time.

When Leslie opened her eyes again, her gaze snapped to Clint's. There was no fear, only determination as she spoke.

"Jacob. I know I can't even imagine the kind of pain you're going through. I get that you want to make me pay for what happened to your wife. But think about what you're doing right now. Are you really going to burn an innocent woman and children to death? They have nothing to do with any of this."

"Shut up!"

He must've pressed the gun against Leslie's head even harder because she flinched and balled up her fists.

Clint continued to breathe evenly, keeping Jacob in his crosshairs. If only he had a clear shot, he'd take it in a heartbeat.

Leslie's eyes snapped open again. She looked at Clint, and while he wasn't sure what she was going to do next, it was clear she was prepared to react if she had the chance.

"Jacob," she began, her voice even. "We both know you don't really want to do this. Come on, put the gun down."

The gunman's brows bunched as pain and anger marched across his face. "I don't care who's in there." He threw the open lighter at the ground by the front door. He must've poured an accelerant there because a fire immediately came alive across the whole entrance. "Just like you didn't care that my Marissa was in that apartment building."

In that moment, Jacob twisted slightly away from Clint, moving the gun from Leslie's head and pointing it at the door of the house.

Clint took in a steady breath, held it, and squeezed off the shot.

Chapter Twenty-Eight

The moment Jacob moved the gun from Leslie's head and started to wave it at the door, she knew it was now or never. She dropped to the ground at the exact same time a gunshot echoed through the night.

She couldn't tell where the shot came from until Jacob's body crumpled to the ground in front of her. His gun hit the pavement and skidded into the grass.

Flames danced as they quickly devoured the kerosene and engulfed the door, side of the house, and the porch railings.

She heard Clint's voice before she saw him approach. He reached a hand down to help her to her feet. "Are you okay?"

"I'm fine. We need the fire department. I can't use a hose on this, not with the kerosene."

"I'm on it." He dialed 9-1-1 on his phone and gave the address. "I need an ambulance and a fire truck at my location. We've got a residential structure fire with three individuals trapped inside."

Clint grabbed Jacob's arm and pulled him away from

the blaze then knelt to put a hand to his neck. There must have been a pulse because he turned the man over and secured his hands behind his back with a pair of handcuffs. "He's alive, but I'm not sure for how long." He retrieved Jacob's gun and put it in his waistband for now.

Leslie pictured her sweet nieces sleeping in their beds, completely unaware of what was going on. And Cindy—the terror of not knowing what was happening to her girls.

"I can't wait, Clint. I'm going in through the back door to get them out."

He gave a grim nod. "Let's go."

At the back door, Leslie reached for a rock nearby and used it to smash the glass. Carefully, she reached through and unlocked it before pulling the door wide open.

The fire alarms were blaring, although the only smoke visible in the kitchen was a thin layer moving along the ceiling as though it were a living creature slowly stalking its prey.

Immediately, they saw that the pantry doors were blocked by the kitchen table. Normally, Cindy might have been able to push the door hard enough to get out, but not if she'd been tied up like Jacob claimed.

Clint put a hand on her shoulder. "I've got Cindy. Go get the girls."

Without hesitation, Leslie dashed down the hallway to Bree's bedroom.

Inside, Izzy was trying to lift her little sister into her arms. "Come on! We have to go!"

Bree covered her ears with her hands, her face wet with tears.

Leslie ran up and scooped Bree into her arms. Izzy whirled around, her sweet little face transitioning from terrified to relieved.

"Auntie! I can't find Mom."

"Officer Clint is getting her. Let's go, girls. We need to get to the backyard. You remember how we talked about meeting at the tree there if there's a fire?"

Izzy nodded. "That way we can find each other."

"That's right." Leslie reached down and took Izzy's hand firmly.

Together, they ran through the house, which was quickly filling with smoke, and out the back door into the cool night air.

"Mom!" Izzy pulled away from Leslie and ran to her mom who was sitting on the ground. Clint stood nearby, part of a rope in his hands.

Cindy pulled the little girl into her arms. "Oh, baby. I'm so glad you're okay."

He dropped the rope on the ground and strode across the grass to pull both Leslie and Bree into a hug.

"Thank God," he breathed.

Sirens split the air.

Clint pressed an urgent kiss to her lips. "I need to go up front and deal with Jacob." He touched her wounded arm where blood had soaked into the sleeve. The stitches had likely been pulled out when Jacob was squeezing her arm earlier.

She nodded. "I'm okay. Go. We're good."

He gave her another kiss then jogged around the edge of the house.

Cindy scrambled to her feet, one arm around Izzy, and stretched her other arm out for Cindy and Bree. Together, they hugged and cried.

Leslie knelt on the cool grass in front of Izzy. "You were such a brave big sister. I have no doubt that, if I hadn't been there, you would've gotten Bree out of the house safely. I'm proud of you."

"Thanks, Auntie." The little girl threw herself into Leslie's arms and then looked up at her mom, who was smiling down at her daughter with pride.

Clint wasn't sure whether or not the hospital had a rule about how many people could be crammed into one room, but if it did, no doubt it'd been broken about six people ago.

Danny Bracken's room was crowded with a bunch of people from the fire department as well as a couple from the police department. Everyone was laughing, swapping stories, and reveling in the relief that the nightmare of the last few days was over.

Had it only been early this morning that Jacob Boulder had been shot and taken into custody? It felt so much longer than that. The bullet Clint fired struck him in the back and had done a fair amount of damage. The doctor operated, and while Jacob was in critical condition, he was expected to make a full recovery.

Clint crossed the room to where Leslie was standing. Her arm was freshly bandaged after a new round of stitches. This time, hopefully it would have a chance to heal.

She looked up at him with a smile and reached for his left hand, lacing their fingers together. That brought on a round of whistles and applause from her co-workers. He pressed a kiss to the back of her hand and grinned.

Detective Paris, who was standing on the opposite side of his room, caught Clint's attention and winked.

Clint reached out and shook Danny's hand. "Glad you're doing so well."

"Me, too. They're releasing me sometime this afternoon."

Becca sank onto the bed next to her husband. "Thank goodness. Everyone here has been great, but I'm ready for my own bed and something to eat besides hospital food." She rested a hand on her expanded belly and laughed.

"I'm sure you are," Bryce spoke up from the back of the room. "We've got a meal train all planned out, with the first delivery tonight for dinner. You shouldn't have to cook for at least a week."

Tears sprang to Becca's eyes. "Thank you. We appreciate you all so much."

Leslie released Clint's hand to give the other woman a hug. They spoke for a moment, but the noise of the room drowned out their words.

A nurse pushed her way into the room. "Okay, okay. We're going to need to break this party up. I've got some vitals to take before we start the discharge process." Even though she spoke in a firm voice, she was all smiles.

"You heard the nice nurse," Bryce's deep voice caught everyone's attention. "Let's give them some space."

They filed out of the room and gathered in the hallway as Leslie's co-workers again told her how glad they were that she was okay.

Chet studied Clint, a serious look on his face. "I heard through the grapevine that you were supposed to have dinner at the station last night."

"I'd been planning on it." Clint reached for Leslie's hand again. "I'm hoping for a raincheck."

Leslie tucked herself against his arm and rested a hand on his chest. "Absolutely. And we're going to keep the teasing to a minimum, right?"

Chet tried to stay serious but failed miserably. He

chuckled. "I'm not going to promise that. But you're welcome at the station anytime."

"Always." Clint carefully put an arm around Leslie's shoulders and steered her toward the elevator. "How are Cindy and the girls?"

Early this morning, Leslie had taken all three of them back to her place to stay until the inspection on Cindy's house was completed and insurance did their thing. Once Clint made sure they were settled, he'd gone back to his house for the rest of the night.

"They're okay. Cindy has some bruising on her wrists and ankles, but otherwise, none of them were hurt. The girls were still asleep when I left. We'll need some things, but Cindy and I'll make a list after I get back."

The elevator doors opened with a ding. They stepped inside and rode it to the ground floor.

Once they exited and were outside, Clint squeezed her hand. "So, we interviewed King again. Once he heard that we'd caught Jacob, he suddenly had no problem talking to us." The security guard had practically begged for a deal if he shared everything he knew. "It turns out that Jacob was going to the same rehabilitation center for grief therapy. That's where he ran into Ortiz. He also saw King accepting a bribe to turn a blind eye to drugs being sold on the center's property. We haven't had the chance to question Jacob yet, but he must have been planning his revenge for a while. When he found out Ortiz had trouble with kleptomania and worked for the same fire station where you were, he figured blackmailing Ortiz would be the best way to net him a set of gear."

Leslie shook her head, a sad look on her face. "Losing a loved one is hard enough to navigate. It breaks my heart that he didn't have the kind of support system he needed." She stopped walking. "I know he's going to serve time, but are there any programs the court can make sure he gets into? Programs that could help him with his grief?"

Her kindness, even toward someone who had made her life such a nightmare these last few days, made Clint proud to know her. "I'm sure there are." He smiled down at her and swept a section of hair behind her ear.

She studied his face, her lips transforming into a smile of her own. "What?"

He tucked her hand into the crook of his arm and led her the rest of the way to her car. Once there, he gently pulled her into his arms. "You're amazing." He kissed the tip of her nose. "I've always thought so. I'm kicking myself for not telling you sooner. I should've asked you out a year or two ago."

"It's okay, because we're here now." She stood on her tip toes and brushed her lips against his. "Which is right where we're supposed to be."

Epilogue
Four Months Later

The sweet baby boy yawned before snuggling into Leslie's arms. How Danny and Becca's little guy managed to stay asleep with all the noise around them, she'd never know. Leslie considered sneaking into Bryce's house and hiding out in one of the rooms so she wouldn't have to relinquish baby Noah to anyone else.

Bryce and Megan had decided to host a barbecue for all their friends and family. Between the fire station and police station, it wasn't a small gathering.

It was a beautiful spring Saturday in mid-March, and their collective group had a lot to celebrate.

An arm gently circled her waist. She turned her head to find Clint watching her, a glimmer in his eyes. He nuzzled her neck and kissed her cheek. "You look happy."

"I am." She reached for one of the baby's hands. His little fingers closed around her thumb. "Isn't he so sweet?"

"You know, I don't think we've had the kid conversation."

"What?" She took her attention off Noah and focused

on her fiancé. "I thought we agreed that we definitely wanted to have kids."

"We did. But we never talked about how many. I mean, I, for one, always thought five would be a nice number."

Five? Leslie's brows rose. "I was thinking more like three."

They studied each other for several moments. The playful smile on his lips coaxed one from her in return.

"Four."

"Four."

They laughed, the sound causing the baby to stir slightly.

Clint rubbed his thumb across the engagement ring on her finger. "I can't wait to marry you, Leslie Granger. October can't come soon enough."

"I can't wait to marry you, either."

Becca approached, touched Leslie's arm, and reached for Noah. "I think we're about ready to eat." She went to stand beside Danny as everyone slowly made their way toward the end of the yard where the smoker and grills were located.

Leslie saw Izzy only a moment before the little girl practically launched herself at Clint. He scooped her into his arms.

She, Cindy, and Bree had stayed with Leslie for several months. Thanks to the quick response of the fire department, Cindy's house had been saved, although repairs to the front and parts of the living room had taken a while. Now they were back in their home again, and Leslie was having to get used to having hers to herself.

"What are you doing, little lady?"

"I'm starving." She put both her hands on her belly, her eyes big. "I can't wait for chicken brisket."

Clint laughed. "Chicken *or* brisket."

Izzy stuck her lower lip out. "I can't have both?"

How could they argue with that? Leslie tickled her niece. "I think you'll have to choose one. Why don't you go ask your mom to help you decide."

Clint set the girl down and laughed again when she ran across the yard to find Cindy.

He turned to Leslie. "What about you?"

"What *about* me?" she asked playfully.

"What are you going to choose?"

Leslie raised her hand and threaded her fingers through the hair at the base of his neck. "You. I'll always choose you."

"Now that's a good answer." He pressed a sweet kiss to her lips. "Does that mean I can have your brisket?"

She smacked him on the chest good-naturedly. "Don't even think about it."

Clint laughed as someone sent out a shrill whistle to get everyone's attention.

Bryce lifted his can of soda. "We have a lot to be thankful for. Weddings," he tipped the can toward Curtis and Rory, who had gotten married a few weeks prior, "engagements," another tip toward Clint and Leslie, "and new life." He motioned toward Danny and Becca with baby Noah. "Goodness knows we've all seen a lot of ups and downs, but one thing is certain. This is a family, whether by blood or choice, that I'm proud to be a part of."

"Hear, hear!"

"Amen to that."

Everyone clapped and raised their drinks together.

"All right. Brisket and chicken will be coming out any minute now. Have fun, enjoy, and try to save some for me."

With a laugh, Bryce traded his drink for a pair of grill tongs and turned toward the smokers.

Clint held his elbow out, and Leslie slipped her arm through his. They had to walk by the tables of desserts to get in line for the main course. Leslie couldn't help but scope out the sweets ahead of time.

Clint leaned in closer, his breath tickling her ear. "Okay, so we know where you stand on the brisket and chicken. But if you had to choose between me and chocolate, which would it be?"

She made a show of thinking over the question. Finally, she stuck out her lower lip much like Izzy had done. "I can't have both?"

That earned her a bark of laughter. "Honey, you can always have both." He captured her bottom lip in a kiss that made her want to forget the whole meal. This man was everything she'd ever wanted—and she'd get to spend her entire life with him by her side. It couldn't get much better than that.

Special Thanks

Wow, it was quite a whirlwind when it came to getting this book finished by the deadline.

Doug, thank you for your encouragement, support, and for staying up with me so many late nights. I love you!

Sydney, thank you for picking up the slack on the household chores, for helping me brainstorm, and for our essential *Alias* breaks. I couldn't have done it without you.

Elizabeth, thanks for cheering me on and for our sprints. We definitely make a good team!

Erynn, I so appreciate you and your editing skills. Thanks for working with me on the timing of this one. You rock!

Steph, Denny, and Alice, you ladies are amazing. Thanks for reading through my book so quickly and offering your advice and suggestions. You are invaluable!

I would especially like to thank all of my readers. This series has been so much fun to write, and it's your encouragement and enthusiasm that made it even better. I'm thankful that we got to go on this adventure together.

Last, but not least, I want to thank my Heavenly Father for His love, never-ending grace, and for the chance to do something I truly love to do.

To Him be the glory!

About the Author

Melanie D. Snitker is a *USA Today* bestselling author who writes inspirational romance and romantic suspense. She and her husband live in Texas with their two children. They share their home with three dogs and two terrariums filled with small critters. In her spare time, Melanie enjoys photography, reading, training her dog, playing computer games, and hanging out with family and friends.

https://www.melaniedsnitker.com/

Books by Melanie D. Snitker

Danger in Destiny

Out of the Ashes

Frozen in Jeopardy

Beneath the Surface

Caught in the Crosshairs

Running from the Past

In Search of the Truth

Assigned to Protect

Surviving the Storm

Forged by Fire

Brides of Clearwater

Marrying Mandy

Marrying Raven

Marrying Chrissy

Marrying Bonnie

Marrying Emma

Marrying Noel

Books by Melanie D. Snitker